Judy Prescott is a 66-year-old widow, originally from Bristol but living in South Wales. She has two grown-up children and five grandsons. Judy started writing in 2014, whilst recovering from breast cancer and hasn't stopped writing since. Initially starting by tracing the family tree and her grandfather's life, she wrote her first book about him and continued from there. This is her 6th book.

I would like to dedicate this book to my late husband,
Adrian, who idolised Elvis Presley.

Judy Prescott

It's Now or Never

AUSTIN MACAULEY PUBLISHERS™

LONDON · CAMBRIDGE · NEW YORK · SHARJAH

A CIP catalogue record for this title is available from the British Library.

ISBN 9781398438910 (Paperback)
ISBN 9781398438927 (ePub e-book)

www.austinmacauley.com

First Published 2023
Austin Macauley Publishers Ltd®
1 Canada Square
Canary Wharf
London
E14 5AA

I would like to acknowledge my family members and friends, who have read this novel before publication, giving honest opinions.

Thank you all.

Chapter One

Ronny settled herself in the corner of the quiet country-style public house, with a large white wine in her hand, earplugs in her ears, listening to music. *It's Now or Never* was playing, a popular song sung by none other than Elvis Presley. Her foot was unconsciously tapping to the tune, her eyes closed and she couldn't have been more laid back if she'd tried.

It had rained the previous day, but today the sun was out in all its glory, and Ronny's mood was energised with the rays from the bright yellow sun above. A free day from work deserved a treat, and her idea of enjoyment had been relaxing with an alcoholic beverage, listening to music, in the atmosphere of the local public house. An afternoon without immediate company, void of any conversation, absolute heaven.

Her job as a nursery nurse kept her busy during the week. With children in her care ranging from babies to four years old, their attention to detail was amazing; Ronny couldn't believe how much their little brains absorbed and how quickly. The smiles on their little faces well outweighed the long days worked, and memories of comical antics of some of the more mischievous beings there were laughable. Going home of an evening, a smile had always erupted as she'd walked through her front door. No one day ever repeated itself.

She would like children of her own some time in her life, she'd decided, but with no boyfriend on the scene, it wasn't about to happen any time soon, or in the near future. Ronny had reached her 30th birthday only a month before, a quiet meal out with her mother and new stepfather.

Her sister now lived in Scotland with her husband and two children and being a committed nurse hadn't been able to join them on the occasion. Peter, her stepfather, had sons, as far as she knew, but any more information of his past hadn't managed to be discussed as yet.

Peter and Margaret, Ronny's mum, had tied the knot only two months earlier: a whirlwind romance, so to speak. They had known each other many moons ago, as friends of friends. Both were married to other partners at the time, Margaret married to Ronny's dad. A chance meeting at Margaret's bakery shop turned into an invitation out, and marriage just six months later.

Ronny couldn't have been more pleased for them but wasn't one to interrogate Peter or interfere with their relationship. She got on with her life, keeping up to date with her mother on regular days out for lunch. The last time they'd met up, before her birthday meal, had coincided with the wedding itself. Nothing fancy, a registry office affair with Ronny and her sister Gina, Margaret's best friend and neighbour Lillian, and Peter's best man Phil. A celebratory meal in the nearby public house, before they'd left for a honeymoon weekend in North Wales.

Money was tight, the bakery shop taking most of Margaret's funds. A continuous struggle, but she'd loved it and soldiered on relentlessly. Cooking had always been her forte, baking cakes, pastries, and decorating anniversary and birthday surprises of excellence. Ronny hadn't inherited her mother's creative mind. Cooking of any sort had no interest to her whatsoever. Gina had also followed in Ronny's footsteps, a caring profession preferred over domestic duties, food preparation at home being mandatory for both of them. Margaret had understood and never forced her passion upon either of them, ever.

Margaret had employed her friend and neighbour, Lillian, to work in her shop. Like her, Lillian loved cooking and between them both, they managed perfectly. Customers became regulars over the years, increasing steadily with their feedback to other potential purchasers, and so on. Both working from home of an evening, preparing culinary delights to supply the shop the following morning, had appeared to be a hobby rather than a chore. New creations were displayed at the counter intermittently before being added as a permanent option to customers, new and old.

There hadn't been much spare time for Ronny and Gina over the years, but neither had complained. Being a single parent, their dad had walked out on the family when they were small children, they hadn't gone without. Margaret's mother, being alive and local at the time, ensured her grandchildren were looked after, whether it was with her or with their own mother. Life was what it was, and not knowing anything different, the sisters were happy as children.

Peter, her new stepfather, became the third "musketeer" delivering the bakery's samples to local offices, working establishments, care homes, etc. during lunch breaks. Readymade sandwiches had added profit potential, an added component to the business and teamwork in triplicate. All were well pleased with their working progress, with happy smiles on everyone's faces.

Peter and Margaret had enjoyed their weekend away in North Wales but were both eager to get back to their bakery shop and business, as usual. Ronny would laugh to herself quietly, their combined commitment exemplary. Their babies reborn, kind of, so enthralling and so focused.

Ronny was quite envious of what they'd had if she'd been honest with herself.

Shaldon was a quiet coastal village, a haven for tourists; small cafés overlooking the bay and the small beach. Quaint shops selling unusual souvenirs, mainly marine-type memorabilia. Anchors, mugs personalised with aquatic scenes, fish ornaments, ships, etc. Fishing rods, nets, buckets and the like. With the small boats inhabiting the area, suitable clothing, fishing bait, all essentials sold for the outdoor experience.

Hard-wearing, outside ornaments to decorate owners' pristine gardens were displayed at the front of terraced properties for all to see and admire. One house actually sold them, the owner a craftsman of the trade and a committed inhabitant who excelled in his skills. A box to insert monies for the objects left outside for perusal and purchasing if they'd been absent from the house for any particular reason. A very trusting community considering today's uncertainty.

A butcher, a baker, but unfortunately, no candlestick maker! A greengrocer, newsagent and Margaret's bakery shop. The essentials required and a little more. One solitary clothes shop, small and boutique-like, expensive too. An unusual souvenir shop, so different from the run of the mill bric-à-brac sold in most seaside towns, selling craft items and glass chess sets all individual and unique. The old-fashioned public houses, so relaxing and tastefully decorated. Fresh fish caught locally cooked to perfection, just one of the favourites on the menu.

Shaldon, in the county of Devon, could be reached by car or by ferry from Teignmouth, another coastal resort nearby. A small rowing boat escorting passengers across the water daily until the tide came in, of an evening. A pittance really, money-wise, for the short journey to the pretty seaside resort. A welcome convenience and part of its charm. Ronny loved living there.

Life in Shaldon rewarded its visitors with a weekly treat during the summer months; a step back in time to the year 1785, with many of the locals dressed for the occasion in period costume. Selling their wares at the small market, dressed in all their finery, or not, as the case may be! Living in the past for all to see and delight in, just pretend but history relived. An experience not to be missed. The village green doubled up for the *Punch and Judy Show*, one for the children and adults alike to watch with roars of hysterics, all enjoying the comical performance. Maypole dancing, an annual festivity, was shown there for all to see. For a small area on the map, it was a hub of festivities, or a peaceful place to relax completely, whichever was the visitors' preference. What wasn't to like about it?

Ronny, immersed in her laid-back afternoon, hadn't realised that she'd been singing along to the music she'd been listening to, as well as tapping her feet in time to the melody, loudly. A tap on her shoulder had caused her to open her eyes and stares from numerous people in the building had her almost cowering in her corner.

'I wouldn't audition for the *X Factor* if I were you,' he said to her, grinning. 'You obviously like Elvis Presley or Rock and Roll, or both.' It was a statement rather than a question.

Ronny hadn't known where to put herself, feeling the blushes on her face with the elevated heat engulfing her body. Knowing she'd to say something, she opened her mouth to speak. He'd beat her to it though, picking up her empty glass and heading for the bar.

'I will get you a refill,' he'd said.

Immediately turning the music off and removing the earplugs completely, Ronny smiled at the captive audience. They slowly reverted to eating their meals, drinking their drinks, and engaging in chitchat with their friends, companions and work colleagues, whatever. She sighed with relief. "Phew" just as the handsome stranger in question had returned with drinks in tow. 'Thank you, I needed that,' she said, sipping from the fresh glass of wine almost immediately.

'My pleasure. You had everyone ogling you, you know. Full marks for the effort though.' He grinned again, wanting to laugh but containing himself.

'I had no idea I was singing aloud, honest. My voice attributes have never been good, ask my mother.' Ronny's chuckle was infectious. The unknown stranger joined in, chuckling on cue.

'I'm Matt, by the way. New around the area and I'm quite liking what I'm seeing so far.' He waited for a response, anything.

'I'm Ronny. Pleased to meet you, Matt, apologies for the voice. I haven't met many locals whose singing is as bad as mine, so don't be put off. Shaldon is lovely, I can assure you.' She was being truthful. The public houses occasionally had a singer or a band for special occasions, but rarely. Otherwise, peaceful existence was what the area was all about. A village so relaxed, it was almost horizontal!

'Glad to hear it. I'm only here for a few days; I live and work in London. What I've seen so far is commendable, everything I'd heard from a relative. You appear to be the exception. What do you do for work? I'm curious,' Matt's eyes studied her intensely, intrigued by the pretty, petite lady sat opposite him.

'I'm a nursery nurse, looking after the babies and toddlers of working parents. Children are hard work, but adorable little beings. I'm lucky in what I do,' she answered. 'Wasn't that what you expected, Matt?'

'I'm not sure what I expected if I'm honest. Working with children requires a strong character and a lot of patience. A sense of fun, too, I would expect,' he paused. 'I'm not familiar with children myself, except my nephew. I don't see much of him as a whole. He lives in America with my brother and sister-in-law.'

'They are miniature versions of us and their determined little minds are contagious. They light up my life as well as wear me out on occasions. Today is my day off, as you've probably guessed. I'm letting my hair down.' Ronny's expression had caused Matt to snigger internally, before heading to the bar for a further refill of alcoholic beverages.

Matt hadn't thought when ordering the drinks. Had Ronny a husband and child of her own?

Was she supposed to be somewhere else soon? Was he being presumptuous or too forward? Slightly guilt-ridden, he returned to the seat apologising as he placed the glasses on the table.

Ronny cleared up the concern in his mind. No, she wasn't married or a mother, and no, he wasn't being too forward. She'd liked his company, even though her plans of spending the day alone, enjoying her own personal space had not been fully realised. As they both walked from the public house, Ronny wished him the best and hoped he would savour her residential area, before returning to London. Waving to each other, they walked in opposite directions, both smiling, never to meet again.

Ronny returned to her small studio apartment, putting the kettle on to boil; a habit rather than an urgent need for a cup of tea. Following in her mother's footsteps, the kettle was constantly on the boil when she returned home after a full day's work. Tea would always be the remedy, the answer to any problem, and therapeutic to the human body. Small parts of the day were put aside, to enjoy a cup of refreshing tea and a biscuit as an added treat.

She settled on the sofa rather than the bed, her cuppa and a chocolate biscuit placed on the small coffee table. Ironically, Ronny would usually have scolded herself for drawing the attention she had in the public house, but instead had felt gratified at how the day had gone. Matt was a ruggedly handsome guy, a good conversationalist and well educated, as far as she could surmise. He would make a more than decent partner and father to somebody. Ronny's chance of meeting up with Matt again was improbable, but she'd relished their one and only meet up. With the television now on, Ronny finished her day off with a relaxing evening tuned into her favourite programmes of the night, a long soak in the bath and reading in bed before sleeping peacefully throughout the remainder of the long-fulfilled day. With a busy session at the nursery the next morning, late nights out were never advisable. The energetic children would require all the enthusiasm she could muster. Miss had needed to be on cue for the gorgeous little darlings.

Margaret had called the next day, on the phone, during her lunch break. She'd wanted a taster for her latest addition to the bakery's counter. An honest opinion, as always. Ronny was usually chief taster for any new recipes, along with Lillian's son, Michael. If both had liked and agreed, new produce enhanced the shop, beginning at the front of the counter, pride of place.

'Okay, Mum. I will call over after work. Do you want me to bring fish and chips from the chippie?' An evening at Margaret's flat usually required the mandatory fish supper, with the resident shop being situated at her end of the village.

'Yes, please. Can you bring an extra portion? We've another taster today. We'll see you tonight. Bye for now, Veronica,' she hung up, allowing her daughter to eat her lunch before work resumed in the nursery.

Ronny wondered who the other taster might be. Her sister hadn't mentioned a visit when they had last spoken. It wasn't school holidays, so the chances of it being her were remote. Jenny and Jonathan, Gina's twins and Ronny's niece and nephew, seldom took time out from school during term time. Lillian did have another son, Martin, so maybe he was joining in, too.

Margaret and Peter lived above the bakery shop, a separate entrance from the shop door itself. The one bedroomed flat was spacious, more so than Ronny's studio apartment. Once Margaret had secured the lease on the shop and flat, years ago, the terraced house shared with her and her sister, Gina, had required forfeiting. Funds couldn't afford both, and with Gina due to move to Scotland for work, Ronny's decision to downsize had been more realistic and more affordable.

It had suited Margaret, living above the shop. Peter added to the business, as well as becoming a new husband and stepfather; the flat was purpose-built and absolutely spot on, ideal, in fact. With room for Peter, as well as Margaret, nothing had required changing. The absence of a garden was compensated with a walk across the road to the village green and relaxing on one of the numerous seats there; when they'd actually found time to relax, that was.

Ronny loved her living location, the large window overlooking the coastal area, the sea, sand, and Teignmouth beyond in clear view. A small balcony, enough for a patio table and two chairs became her viewpoint and area for putting everything into perspective when weather permitted. A relatively simple life, but one she couldn't complain about and one she'd loved, so she'd thought. The children were now back with their parents, the nursery cleared of toys, books, crayons, etc, items scattered all around the large room picked up, the floor surpassing the hygiene inspection after a thorough brush and mop clean. New learning toys in preparation for the little darlings (or devils) the following day were in place, so Ronny's day had ended. She left the nursery and headed for the local chippie for the fish supper at her mother's flat and chief cake taster.

Having a spare key to the flat above the bakery shop, Ronny let herself in and climbed the set of stairs to the front door. The main door wasn't locked and knocking before entering, her usual approach, she carried the fish supper carefully and placed it on the worktop in the kitchen. The room was empty, but voices were heard in the lounge, several voices.

The look on Ronny's face was one of shock horror as she entered the room. It was Margaret, her mum, that had spoken first.

'Veronica, this is Peter's son, Matthew. He's come for a short visit.'

Ronny was gobsmacked, pleased and excited, all at the same time. Her mind was full of bewilderment, so much so that she couldn't speak. It was Matt's voice she'd then heard.

'Pleased to meet you, Veronica.' His words were said calmly, but his face had shown pure devilment. The hint of a smile forming across his mouth though, a while later, had caused Ronny to smile, too.

Chapter Two

Margaret returned to the kitchen with her husband, plating the fish suppers up for everyone. Lillian and her son, Michael, were seated on the large sofa deep in conversation, something personal between them both. Ronny hadn't wanted to interrupt.

'You're definitely a Ronny more than a Veronica,' Matt said to her, winking.

'Likewise, Matt suits you much better than Matthew,' Ronny's stern criticism hadn't been expected.

'Touché. I deserved that!' Matt was howling now, hysterically.

Margaret and Peter both walked into the room carrying plates containing their meals, as Matt's cackle had erupted.

'What's the joke, Matthew?' Peter asked quizzically.

'Nothing much, Dad. That's between Ronny and me.' Matt was still in stitches, infectious laughter, causing Ronny to join in. The stares only heightened the duplicated hysteria.

The food was delicious, all swallowed down quickly with plenty of liquid refreshment, cups of hot tea. The chippie had never disappointed, always perfectly cooked, with the fish's batter outstanding and unique. Ronny frequently opted for battered sausage and chips, or corned beef rissole, rather than cook herself a meal in her apartment, of an evening. Laziness probably at times, but after a hard day at work, well deserved.

Now for the tasting: Margaret brought in the new cake concoction; a red velvet sponge decorated with black cherries and a rich buttercream topping. It had looked delicious, too good to cut up and eat. The presentation was first class. Margaret prepared five slices on individual plates, offering single cream as an accompaniment. Forks were offered to everyone, and the tasting began. The silence was deafening, you could hear a pin drop. As the plates became empty and silence remained, Margaret eventually spoke.

'Well! What's the verdict?'

'Mum, it's scrumptious and moreish,' Ronny replied honestly. Lillian and Michael both agreed, and Peter nodded in total agreement.

'Matthew?' Peter asked. 'What do you think?'

'I need another slice to make a decision,' he responded. 'Seriously though, ten out of ten, Margaret.'

'All agreed then. I will start making it tomorrow for the shop the following day. Thanks all. Another cuppa anyone?' she asked, looking around the room.

'I thought you'd never ask, Margaret,' replied Matt and sat down on one of the dining chairs.

'You're incorrigible, you know that,' said Ronny looking directly at him, smirking.

As Margaret and Peter returned to the kitchen to boil the kettle for a second cup of tea, they engaged in small talk, discovering unknown things about each other, little things. Matt asked after the children at the nursery, and whether they had behaved themselves today. Ronny was about to reply when the tea presented itself.

'Am I missing something here, Veronica? Do you know each other?' Ronny's mother was curious.

'Sort of, Mum,' she blurted out before looking at Matt. 'It's complicated.'

Ronny's mother gave up, shrugged her shoulders and headed towards the sofa where Lillian and Michael were seated. Conversing with Lillian about the new addition to the shop counter, Peter joined in the conversation too, leaving Michael to happily sup his tea in complete silence. He wasn't a talker, very private and a little aloof at times, though not purposely. It was just his character, a loner, a mummy's boy, and still living at home at 30 years of age. Both Ronny and Michael were in the same class at school. She knew him well enough, although Martin, his brother had been an unknown entity. He lived away somewhere now, not a frequent visitor. Ronny recalled the more attractive brother, two years older than her, and wondered about him.

Leaving the youngsters to talk among themselves, Matt asked whether Ronny was free on Saturday morning for a coffee, before he headed back to London. It was now Thursday, so work as usual on Friday, but no commitments on the weekend at all were in her diary. She accepted, before asking where he was staying.

'The Ness!' she shouted. 'You're staying at The Ness. I've always wanted to take a look inside the rooms in that hotel. The higher up, the better. I'm so envious.'

'It's a date, then. Meet me after breakfast at the hotel and I will give you a tour,' Matt smiled.

'You're on.' Ronny high-fived him with her hands, shouting with glee.

The looks from the others could have swallowed them up, and Ronny almost cowered as she'd done in the public house a day earlier. Matt shrugged his shoulders, ignoring the stares.

Walking back to her apartment, Ronny slapped herself hard. Had all that really happened tonight? She'd suddenly felt like a teenager again, eyeing up the opposition with her sister.

Teignmouth had been where the nightlife was, and where the sisters had spent many an evening looking for their match. Margaret would pick them up in the early hours of the morning, or organise a taxi to take them home.

Gina had met her future husband there, he'd spent a vacation in Teignmouth with his best friend and Gina had been smitten, instantly. Alistair's male companion, James, had tried to connect with Ronny, but there hadn't been any chemistry there. She'd no interest in him at all, though as a person nothing detrimental was obvious. Gina and Alistair met on their own later in the week; the rest is history.

Studying to become a nurse, Gina had managed to obtain a place in Edinburgh to finish her degree and be with Alastair. She, unlike Ronny, hadn't worried about leaving the village and everything it had represented. Her boyfriend was in Scotland, where she wanted to be. A busy city, she'd gotten used to the new environment, the constant traffic on the roads, and the lack of peaceful solitude; Ronny lived for the latter, a busy city wouldn't appeal. Her worst nightmare, probably.

Matt had that something; something that had caused her heart to race, her mind to wander and a definite need to see him again. Not boyfriend material, maybe a friend who was a boy! She was excited at the prospect of meeting up at the hotel on Saturday, The Ness, no less. She'd not let on that her studio apartment was located minutes away from it. He hadn't needed to know, yet.

Matt had walked to the hotel after Ronny had left her mother's flat (she still couldn't call it her parents' home. Peter wasn't her father and never would be). The slower than usual walk had him in a quandary. What was it with this lady, Veronica or Ronny, her name hadn't mattered. She had somehow held intrigue, a compulsion to get to know her better. A sudden roar erupted after remembering the first time they had met, in the small public house. Matt had never before imposed on a lady, a stranger at that, and connected quite so attentively.

She preyed on his mind that night, causing a restless sleep, not usual for him. Matt walked onto the balcony of his room, gazing up at the stars in the sky. The sea, calm and yet mesmerising, no beach in view. The tide had swallowed it all up for the time being, and the silence was awe-inspiring. It had held an ambience about it, something elusive. A natural occurrence, yet hypnotic. Matt suddenly realised the magic of the coast, something London couldn't compete with.

After drinking a hot cup of tea on the balcony, gazing at the stars with fascination, Matt finally slept. He'd changed though; a certain lady had managed to absorb him completely. Matt had a fiancé back in London, one he'd loved dearly. Rose was his world, but Ronny was playing games with his conscience, his mind, his everything, and he'd no idea why. Ronny woke earlier than normal on Saturday morning. She was excited at meeting Matt, but more so at being shown around the hotel that had the most spectacular views over the coast and was prominently placed for exclusive clientele due to its highly priced tariff. She had enjoyed a latte coffee sat outside on the balcony area on occasional summer days, when open to non-residents. Intrigued to know what had warranted such a high charge for staying there, Ronny was so looking forward to the tour. Whether she'd been able to afford to stay there was irrelevant, being a working-class girl at heart she wouldn't allow herself to part with the kind of cash they commanded, when a longer break elsewhere could equally match their prices.

Dressed casually in denim jeans and a loose long-sleeved blouse, her hair pulled back in a scruffy ponytail, Ronny had no intention of pretending she was anyone but herself. Walking across the road to where she'd espied Matt waiting outside the entrance to the hotel, she smiled and waved. He looked as handsome as she'd remembered, and Ronny had really looked forward to the meet up if she'd been honest. An invitation for a coffee and a chat, but in a place, she'd never expected to experience.

Heading the way through the front entrance, Matt walked slowly enough for her to take it all in. The foyer was laid out in a well-organised fashion, but there were no high ceilings or clear crystal chandeliers, something she'd always envisaged being there. Why, she'd not known, the image in her head had prominent features since being a teenager, she was sorely disappointed. The dining room was decorated to a high standard; pure white tablecloths covering numerous tables, set at two, four and six place settings. All very neat and exact, she was impressed.

Entering the lift to the top floor, Matt headed towards his room as they'd exited the lift and walked the short journey through the hallway. The décor there was conservative, clean and clutter-free. A few paintings hung evenly spaced on the walls, both sides, images of soothing coastal scenes from local artists. Nothing spectacular, but not tacky either. Creating a tranquil image for the hotel, Ronny was pleased with their personal choice.

As Matt opened the door to his room, she walked in ahead of him. He was already packed for the return journey home, the evidence on his already made four-poster bed. Looking around the good-sized room, the built-in wardrobe, large desk, and huge television mounted on the wall opposite the bed, Ronny's eyes espied the balcony.

First, though, she headed for the en suite bathroom, poking her head inside curiously. Looking at Matt, she said to him, 'Where's the Jacuzzi bath and his and hers matching sinks? For the prices they charge, it should be standard for every room.'

Matt roared with laughter before replying, 'You really are an innocent village girl, Ronny. I so like that about you.'

'Why, thanks for that. I will take that as a compliment. Can I take a look from the balcony, please?' she asked politely.

'No problem. It's the best bit as I discovered last night.' Matt had been serious. The views were spectacular in the darkness, unbelievable.

Walking onto the largish area, Ronny held onto the ornate metal railings and gazed towards the scenic views ahead, amazed. 'Wow, seeing this makes the expense all worth it. I thought the view from my apartment was good, but this definitely tops it, no question.'

'Do you live far from here then?' Matt asked inquisitively.

'Across the road, five minutes' walk away. This is better, much better. I feel I want to paint the scenery, if I could paint, that is,' Ronny laughed loudly. 'If only! Matchstick men are about my limit.'

'How about that coffee before I head home?' Matt said, indicating the exit from the room.

The bar area coupled up as a café on cold days. Dark furnishings and soft lighting created a calming ambience, and tables were spaced far enough apart to allow privacy between groups of visitors staying in the hotel. Ronny sat at a small table overlooking the bay as Matt ordered the coffees at the bar. Their time spent together was very relaxed, small talk, nothing serious. She thanked him for allowing her to snoop around the hotel, one of her guilty pleasures.

As they both walked out of the main door, Matt, with his suitcase in his hand, thanked her for her company. Promising to see her around soon, he headed for the car park and his journey home.

Ronny waved as he drove down the hill towards the exit out of Shaldon itself. A smile adorned her face, but internally, she was a little sad. There was definitely something about Matt that had instantly appealed to her. Maybe not romantically, but she had wanted him in her life, permanently.

Recalling their conversation afterwards, Ronny hadn't found out anything about Matt really, nothing of significance anyway. She still didn't know how old he was, whether he was single, married or in a relationship. She knew he had a married brother in America from their previous conversation and a nephew. Had he any other siblings, though? Was his mother still living?

Questions on her mind, too many.

Nothing had been divulged on Ronny's front either, apart from her full name, Veronica Vivienne Johnson, and her

27

sister's name Virginia Victoria Clarke (nee Johnson), affectionately known as Gina to Ronny and her close friends. Ronny's mother always referred to the girls using their true Christian names, a stickler of habit. If anyone had called her Maggie, Meg, Marge, or any other name commonly linked with the name Margaret, her facial expression would show a complete disregard to anything other than her birth name, and they would automatically revert to her true name without hesitation.

'If I'd wanted to call you Ronny, it would be registered on your birth certificate, Veronica.' A conversation her mother had often had with her, causing continuous smirks from Ronny herself. 'It's not funny, Veronica.' Ronny could laugh about it now, and did, on numerous occasions.

Matt's criticism of her name and indeed, her sister's had contributed to a conversation about Christian names in general. Going through every name under the sun, he'd wanted to know her father's name.

The laugh had been expected even before the words were spoken. 'Dad's name is Vernon.' Expecting Matt to reciprocate with Christian names on his side of the family, nothing was forthcoming, nothing at all. So, the topic changed to places visited throughout the years. Matt was a traveller, for sure, enjoying long-distance adventures when vacating, remote holiday islands especially. Not your typical European countries, Spain, Portugal, Greece, etc. His idea of a holiday involved water sports, skiing, paragliding and mountaineering. Ronny had screwed her nose up at the thought of it, all much too energetic for her.

Ronny had never ventured very far afield. Cornwall, Wales, all pretty local really. She had travelled to France one year with her sister, an urge to visit the Eiffel Tower, for why she'd not known, but a box ticked on her wish list somewhere down the line. Never envious of others' escapades, a few days relaxing locally in a moderately priced hotel or static caravan, suited her down to the ground. Not wanting anything above her means, she was more than happy with her lot.

The previous day's frivolities played on Ronny's mind the next day. A Sunday, a day off work, she usually cleaned her apartment in the morning, before going for a stroll in the afternoon, weather permitting. The small zoo, where exotic creatures were on show to visitors all over the world, often had her spending a few hours there, followed by a pub lunch in one of the local public houses. The animals and birds knew her well, and she conversed with them as if they were human beings.

Sometimes, a delicious cream tea in their small café had sufficed.

Not wanting to impose on her mother and stepfather and their one and only day off from the bakery shop, they hadn't needed a visit from her, not in her mind anyway. As newlyweds, they'd deserved time to themselves during the day. Evenings were spent in the kitchen baking, in preparation for the next days' cooking delights for their customers.

Peter had taken over the paperwork side of things, ordering essential foods she'd not cooked. Sliced bread, bread rolls, paninis. Single and double cream, clotted cream (Devon's favourite), not forgetting the squirty cream. Strawberries, when in season, and various other fruits and vegetables were ordered on a regular basis. Sandwich fillers for the offices, care homes and working establishments, Peter's baby!

Small pots of assorted jams to accompany the plain and fruit scones Margaret regularly displayed. Ronny loved the cheese variation and often pinched a few to take home with her. She ignored her mother's scathing looks, knowing she'd not minded really. Savoury before sweet, Ronny's preference. Although, some of her mother's regular sweet fancies had her drooling, being so mouth-watering and delicious.

That afternoon, her mind reverted back to her father, Vernon. He was actually named Vernon Victor Johnson, after his father and his father before him. An only child, there had been no one else to carry the *V*s down the line. Margaret, her mother, and her dad had ensured the line continued, and Gina's twins were christened Violet Jennifer and Victor Jonathon, but known by their middle names. If Ronny ever had children in the future, the thought of finding a V name for a son or daughter, or both, was daunting, mind-blowing, in fact.

Chapter Three

Ronny and Gina's dad had left the family home when they were young children, five and seven years respectively, Ronny being the younger of the two. He'd returned to his hometown of Exeter, not coping well with the quietness of the small village life in Shaldon. Margaret had been born and bred there but had moved to Exeter on their marriage, where his roots and his job was at the time. Margaret hadn't settled at all, though not for the want of trying. The girls kept her busy enough, but she'd not been happy and it had shown. Agreeing to move to Shaldon, Vernon focused on work in the small community, not earning megabucks but enough to keep the family fed and watered, so to speak. Her mother had found plenty to do, what with the girls and her love of baking.

Ronny's grandmother lived locally too, so popping round to see her was a normal daily occurrence.

The marriage disintegrated solely because of her dad's boredom, his inability to cope with living in a small close-knit community. He so relished being back in Exeter, among the built-up traffic, busy environment, and the noise that was normal for city life; the one thing Margaret had abhorred. Their needs were oh so different, and sadly, Ronny's dad moved back to his roots alone, where he'd felt he had belonged.

He'd distanced himself ever since, not wanting to upset his girls too much. The odd birthday card, with monies inside, was indeed irregular and eventually stopped completely, nothing coming at all. Ronny would never forget him; he was and still is her dad. The breakdown of her parents' relationship was unavoidable. He was a city boy and she was a village girl, through and through. Their future was doomed from the start.

Sadly, Ronny had missed out on her dad's family after the separation, her grandparents' particularly. She'd loved her grandmother, the lady who had spoiled her and her sister when visiting; all to her mother's dismay and detriment, she had killed them with kindness and Ronny was so glad that she had, losing touch with her for so many years now. Her grandfather wasn't well the last time she'd seen him, and she wondered whether he was still around today.

Suddenly, it had become important to know where her dad was and to communicate with him again. Why? She'd been unsure. After two decades of no contact, the timing appeared to be right, now. What had Matt done to her? Her feelings were all over the place, completely out of sync.

Ronny's mind had rewound itself back to her childhood and happy memories of a fully functional family. One with a mother and a father: all living together in harmony.

Exeter hadn't held many memories for her, being so young before moving to Shaldon; her grandparents hadn't been forgotten, they had stood there in front of her now. She could see them quite clearly. Pride of place, they were, as if it was only yesterday. An older version of her dad, the resemblance between him and her grandfather was striking.

Matt, an unknown specimen less than a week beforehand, had elevated her senses, and her areas of importance. He had unknowingly, at such an early stage in her life become permanent. Matt was, in every sense of the word, her stepbrother, due to a recent marriage, her mother's. A person she'd known absolutely nothing about but was determined to find out a lot more.

His dad, Peter (her stepfather) had been a friend of Vernon's (her dad) in years gone by; a volcano had suddenly erupted after living dormant in her mind for years. Her concerns regarding her own father and his family now ignited. Ronny hadn't wanted to question her mother and stepfather directly, but with Matt's help, maybe her dad could be reunited with his not-so-little girls again, just maybe!

The Elvis Presley song that had brought Matt and Ronny together echoed in her ears, without any rhyme or reason. *It's Now or Never.*

Ringing her mother later on in the evening, Ronny had asked for Matt's telephone number.

Margaret's response hadn't appeared helpful; nothing new to her really.

'Why do you want that? You do know he is your stepbrother, Veronica?' Margaret's stern response was full of intrigue.

'Of course, I do, Mum. We seem to get on well, there's something I want to ask him, that's all,' Ronny replied.

'Hold on, I will ask Peter now.' The line had become quiet for a few minutes.

With the number written down, she thanked her mother and rang off. Margaret was one of little words. Ronny knew she had cared, but conversation for conversation's sake wasn't her mother, not at all, and never had been. She'd no time to waste on unneeded small talk.

Matt would still be relaxing after travelling home the day before, she'd surmised. Would it hurt to ring him now, whilst everything was reeling in her mind? *It's Now or Never*, played itself again in her head, so she pressed the numbers given before bottling out completely.

A female voice answered the phone, not something Ronny had expected. Maybe he was married had quickly entered her mind. It had halted her initial opening lines, throwing her off balance, off the track completely.

'Hi, I'm wondering whether I could speak to Matt, please. I'm his stepsister, Ronny. We both met recently,' she said quietly, hoping not to cause any upset.

'Oh, hello there. I'm Rose, Matt's fiancé. He's told me a lot about you,' the lady replied.

'Oh, all good, I hope. Our first meeting up was a bit bizarre, embarrassing on my part.' Ronny had no idea what Matt had told her about everything and hoped he'd not made her a laughing stock.

'Absolutely, being one of three boys, he's excited about bonding with a sister, even through marriage,' Rose replied, excited and completely calm.

'I'm so glad. I'm asking for a favour from him if he's available. It's been lovely talking to you, Rose.' Ronny had meant it, every word.

Matt had answered the phone with an enlightened mood, obviously used to travelling for a living, and well used to pressure. She'd still not known what his career had entailed. Ronny mentioned her father, and how she'd wanted to rekindle their relationship. Wanting him to do some investigating, without being too obvious, he'd agreed wholeheartedly.

'Leave it to me, Sis,' he'd said. 'You deserve to know him again. I will talk to my dad soon, and hopefully, Rose and I can take a weekend off work in the near future when we can meet up and bring you both together.'

'Thank you so much, Matt, I would like that. This is all your fault, you know. I hadn't wanted to resurrect the past until now. Mum and Peter mustn't know though, not yet anyway.' Ronny had been serious. Something had happened to her since meeting Matt. Such a jovial character on the outside, he was on her side. The quiet Veronica, Margaret's choice of endearment, somehow wanted to be heard! And she'd loved being called sis, too.

Life resumed to normality, with work at the nursery, visits to the bakery shop during business hours and relaxing in her apartment. The chippie had received quite a few visits during the week, with no interest in cooking herself a meal. She was living on a knife-edge, eager for news on her father's whereabouts and the weeks were flying by. Matt's call couldn't come soon enough. Her regular monthly midweek day off was due in a few days, and she'd deliberated as to what to do with her well-deserved break.

Ringing her mother that night, Ronny had suggested an evening out in Teignmouth with Peter, on that particular day. A change from the normal everyday routine, and a chance to find out more about her elusive stepfather, if she'd trod carefully enough, that was. Margaret had agreed, mentioning a restaurant there that she'd liked for its delicious food choice.

'Okay. I will book it up now. Any more new ideas for the bakery, Mum?' Another tasting session had sounded like a good idea.

'No, not really. Unless you've any bright ideas for a new recipe, that is. Feel free to enlighten me, Veronica,' Margaret was asking.

'Well, I do have one idea, Mum. When Matt took me to The Ness for a nose about, we had coffee and mini Welsh cakes. Maybe a pack of 12 mini ones to take away. They would be lovely with a cup of tea at home, and if The Ness can serve them, then you can sell them,' Ronny suggested. 'Peter can include them on his regular lunch break deliveries, too.'

'That's a brilliant idea, Veronica. How come you've only now mentioned it? It was weeks ago that you were there,' her mother responded.

'It's only just occurred to me. It could also work with other cakes, mini jam tarts maybe. I'm going now; I will speak to you soon.' Ronny hung up, putting the kettle on to boil. Where that had come from, she'd no clue. In retrospect though, it had been a light-bulb moment, one of her better suggestions.

With the phone number handy for the restaurant, she booked a table for eight o'clock, giving everyone plenty of time to get ready. Margaret and Peter didn't venture out often even on their own. It would be a treat for them, as much as Ronny, and her mother had received plenty of notice to double up on supplies the evening before, for the bakery shop's counter.

The children had kept her busy during her work shift, always. Miss had high regard for two of the little boys there, Ben and Aaron, three-year-old twins. They were adorable, blue-eyed, blonde-haired, compulsively huggable toddlers. Mischievous and talkative, their dad had worked away a lot, and their mum was high up in school affairs, she'd not known much more than that. Money was no object, but Ronny had felt that they'd not received a lot of attention when back home. The contact she'd had with them hadn't convinced her that they were loved as much as she had cared for them.

Ronny had never met their father, they were always picked up by their mother and conversation was short and sweet before leaving the nursery. If the mother hadn't been available, a neighbour would pick them up. Daddy had often had a drawing of him done, always alone, attempted by the twins. A three-year-old version of their father and his pet dog, Rufus. Any pictures of their mother, with the boys, hadn't included their dad or the dog. A bit odd, but Ronny was talking about three-year-old children in general here.

Miss had Ben and Aaron in tears one afternoon when discussing the school holidays, wondering whether Mummy and Daddy were taking them away for the half-term week. The nursery had remained open for the duration, but the majority of the children had enjoyed a reprieve on school breaks. Time to gel with their families, their little souls full of enthusiasm about their adventures and stories about their escapades on their return. The twins, since starting nursery hadn't seemed to venture out and about that much. They'd both enjoyed their time with the other children at the nursery though, something Ronny was more than grateful for.

There was bound to be favourites among the little darlings, though Ronny had tried not to show it. She had a special soft spot for the twins; they seemed to cling to her when she was around. Looking after children of all ages had rewarded her with the status of Miss, and she loved it, feeling so important.

It was her day off, and Ronny slept in for a change, getting up much later than usual. Feeling guilty, Ronny cleaned the apartment thoroughly, whiling away a few hours. A cup of tea, toast and strawberry jam and watching the television light heartedly, not really focused on the programmes at all. A soak in the bath afforded soft music wafting from the main living area, and Ronny, for once in her life, had suddenly felt alone. She hadn't known why, always satisfied with her own company as a rule; in fact, insisting on it, feeling safer alone. Not now, though.

Matt's intervention had made her realise that a relationship, or rather male company on any level, wasn't a disaster waiting to happen. After the time spent with him, not a lot, in reality, she'd felt truly comfortable conversing with Matt. A jovial personality, discovering he was indeed her stepbrother was a relief and also a huge surprise. He had stirred up an ignited response to male companionship, a fear she seemed to have had for many years, for some unknown reason, nothing that had sprung to mind though. Ronny had never avoided the male person intentionally but had avoided a relationship outside a long-established friendship.

Ronny had willed Matt to ring with any information he had discovered, but nothing, nothing at all. Disappointed, Ronny would admit, but hopefully, he would find out something sometime soon. On the plus front, she now knew that there was not one, but three stepbrothers about. Would she get to see the other two any time? Rose had sounded a lovely person on the phone, meeting her would be nice, too. Ronny had suddenly felt the need to spread herself about a little, rather than living in the sheltered bubble she'd been in for years. All her own doing, admittedly.

The phone hadn't rung, and so she dressed for the meal out with her mother and stepfather.

People didn't dress up these days, always tidy, but apart from special occasions, a clean set of clothes had sufficed. A taxi from theirs would take them all to the restaurant, and return them later that evening. Ronny was happy to walk back in the dark from her mother's afterwards, without any fear at all. Shaldon's crime history was bearing on nil; she'd not heard anything sinister occurring. The odd teenage scuffle, some graffiti damage through sheer boredom, but Shaldon remained relatively unscathed throughout the years.

Strolling the short walk to the bakery shop's flat, Ronny's perspective on life had suddenly changed. At 30 years of age, she'd wanted more communication outside of work and had decided that she was going to do something about it. Colleagues at work had regularly invited her out for casual drinks and evening meals, both male and female. Ronny had always refused their numerous invitations and eventually, they had stopped asking, it had been inevitable really. She'd always had the illusion of being more than comfortable in her life, but Matt had given her cause to somehow doubt herself.

The newlyweds were ready when Ronny had got to their flat, a taxi was due in five minutes. Margaret was as organised as ever. The kitchen worktop was full to brimming with her mother's cooking: pastries, pies and perfectly baked scones of all variations. A birthday cake in the shape of a unicorn, intricately decorated with rainbow icing, and the number five visible for all to see.

'Wow, that's gorgeous. Whose birthday is it?' Ronny asked inquisitively. 'You're so clever, Mum.' Ronny studied it again; the details were spot on, absolutely perfect. Her mother had a lot of patience where creative work was required.

'Little Abbie at number 6, her mother passed away last year, and her father's been off the scene since her birth. She lives with her grandparents now. Come on, the taxi is here!'

It had only taken ten minutes to get to the restaurant, and Ronny could have walked the journey easily enough. No doubt, the other two could have too, but walking had never been their passion, not her mother's anyway; Peter's preferences were still an unknown entity. Ronny had never complained, going along with the flow, not a person to argue with anyone, completely out of character. Until now that was. Matt had brought the devil out in her, for some peculiar reason.

'Maybe on my next midweek day off we can walk into Teignmouth, Mum. If Lillian is willing to hold the fort for a few hours, that is.' The look on her mother's face had said it all. 'It was only a suggestion.'

Peter had paid the taxi driver, giving him a time to pick them up again. He'd noted it in his diary and drove away. Entering the restaurant, a pub-style establishment, Ronny immediately felt at home. She'd not recalled ever visiting it and asked her mother whether she'd indeed been there before. Familiar, some areas she'd recognised. Knowing the way to the conveniences, how had she known?

'As young children, yes. Your dad and I used to bring you here often. The place hasn't changed that much.'

'That's why I immediately felt at home here. Where's the menu, I'm starving.' She'd recalled only eating toast and jam all day, no wonder. Not enough to feed a sparrow had come to mind.

Ronny had suddenly giggled.

'What, Veronica? What's so funny?' her mother asked.

She spat out the reason for her giggles, whilst still giggling, and Margaret suddenly lightened up and a smile lit her face. She was an attractive lady when she smiled.

'Yes. I remember that phrase well. It was Virginia who had the appetite, you were the picky one. Getting food down you at times caused stern disagreements between your dad and me.'

With her dad getting a mention, Ronny dared ask the question lurking in the back of her mind. 'Do you know where Dad is living, Mum? I'd like to try and reconnect with him, if possible. I'm a big girl now!' There, she'd said it.

'I don't know exactly, but he's still in Exeter somewhere. Why now, Veronica?'

'I'm suddenly feeling a little isolated. You've got Peter for company now, so I'm not in demand so much. Matt's fault entirely, I blame him. He's such a character, I connected with him immediately, as a brother nothing more, Mum.' She'd needed to put that matter straight before continuing. 'I'm wondering about Dad now and would like to see him again.'

'I will see what I can do, Veronica, Ronny, whatever you call yourself now,' her mother replied, loosening up for a change.

Ronny was taken aback momentarily and hugged her, not a natural occurrence usually. 'Thanks, Mum, and it's Ronny, please.'

The meal was delicious. The steak was tender and cooked to perfection, the peppercorn sauce exactly right. Mushrooms, onion rings, a half tomato grilled and fat homemade chips, lots of them.

All three of them had ordered identical meals from the menu. Ronny rubbed her belly afterwards, drank her white wine and sighed.

'That was just what the doctor ordered!' she informed them.

Peter had laughed then, never seeing her so laid back before, and telling her so. Ronny's roar was heard throughout the whole establishment.

'Ronny, please. You're drawing attention to yourself.' Her mother's words echoed in her ear.

'Not for the first time either. That's how Matt and I met. I was drawing a lot of attention then.' She told them her story and to the "oldies" it had made complete sense. The joke about their names at the flat, when tasting Margaret's red velvet cake and single cream, the constant giggles between them later, and the instant connection between the two.

Margaret had sighed relief, it had shown all over her face. Why, she'd not a clue. They were stepchildren, not remotely related and were allowed to have a serious relationship if things had gone that way, but it hadn't.

'So, Rose says you have two other sons, Peter. Matt mentioned a brother in America, so where is the third one?' It was an easy enough question to answer.

'He's still in Exeter, where I'm from, but his business isn't going well at the moment. He's in the food industry too and owns a restaurant. He's the head chef there. He's seriously thinking about selling up and moving down here. There are a few vacant properties in Teignmouth that could be turned into a decent eatery quite easily, at a reasonable cost.' Peter's information had surprised her. Ronny hadn't uttered a word. Her jaw dropped and Margaret tapped her on the shoulder.

'Shut your mouth, Veronica, I mean Ronny. You're causing another scene.'

It was Peter that had giggled then, before turning to his wife. 'Lighten up, darling. It's nice to see her in good humour.'

'If he's anything like Matt, I look forward to meeting him,' Ronny had then said.

'They are identical twins and very similar in character,' Peter informed her, causing Ronny's reaction equalling the one before. His hysterical outburst had Margaret not knowing where to turn.

Picking up the dessert menu, Ronny chose her favourite, chocolate fudge cake and cream. 'There's another idea, Mum. Mini chocolate fudge cake squares!'

With the evening concluded, Ronny walked back to her apartment, carrying a bag full of cheese, plain and fruit scones; a carton of clotted cream and two small pots of jam, her mother concerned that she wasn't eating enough. A huge smile adorned her face and she'd have whistled all the way home if she'd been able to whistle. Ronny had felt alive. The reclusive nobody was coming out of her shell, and about time, too.

Chapter Four

Matt had received a phone call the following evening. This time it was him who had answered, rather than Rose.

'Well. hello there, Sis. How are things in sleepy Shaldon? Apologies for not being in touch.'

'As good as it gets. I'm on the Vernon Victor Johnson trail finally and things are looking up, at last.' Ronny was serious. 'How are things in smoky London?'

'Ditto! Rose is pregnant, but you're sworn to secrecy. We're coming down for the weekend, both of us. I've done some investigating as well and have a few pointers regarding your dad's whereabouts. All will be revealed then,' Matt's humour was infectious and his snigger was incorrigible. Ronny couldn't even begin to think about him having an identical twin, the images creating havoc in her head.

'Are you staying in The Ness again?' It was a question she'd already known the answer to.

'Absolutely, where else would I stay? If you get your easel and some paints, the balcony is all yours for the matchstick men masterpiece,' he roared with laughter.

'Funny, ha, ha, Matt. I tried whistling last evening after a meal out with your dad and my mum, couldn't manage that either.' Ronny could tell Matt anything without getting embarrassed.

'Letting your hair down at last. How are the "oldies" by the way?'

'They are both fine. I actually got a smile from Mum last night, at my expense though. I'm getting good at making a fool out of myself,' Ronny replied. 'It's good to hear from you, Matt. I'm looking forward to the weekend and my lips are sealed.'

'We will see you all soon. Bye for now.' Matt ended the call.

Ronny's face had felt as if it was about to crack, due to all the smiles and laughter incurred recently. Her skin hadn't known how to cope with it all. A large dab of moisturising cream had penetrated her face that night before bedtime, in the hope of stopping the dry chapped exterior that had begun to erupt. The pitfalls of life, but a few extra wrinkles along the way in the search for happiness were more than welcome, temporarily.

Ronny, at work, appeared to relax more than usual. The children were little angels the majority of the time, but minor accidents due to hurried play, the occasional argument over two children wanting the same toy and sibling rivalry were all too common. Ben and Aaron, one particular afternoon had caused concern. Not acting like the cheeky little monkeys around her, normal for them, their sombre looks had shown sadness.

Pulling them to one side, Ronny asked if they were okay. At first, neither of them responded, until Ben had started to cry, that was. Hugging him tightly, he spoke, so upset.

'Mummy's leaving us and moving to another house. Daddy said we can still see her, but it will only be Daddy and Rufus in our house.'

Ronny's surprised facial expression had caused Aaron to speak then. 'We are still coming here with you, Miss. Daddy said so!' Suddenly Aaron started crying.

For three, almost four-year-olds, the twins were intelligent beings and so much older than their years. They were also children of tender age and she'd hated seeing them so unhappy. Not living far from her mother's bakery shop, Ronny had recalled the beautiful birthday cake she'd made a few days earlier.

'Listen to me carefully, both of you. You know little Abbie, she was five years old recently, well, she lives with her grandma now. She's doing okay and likes living there. You'll be good with your dad, too.' Trying to convince them, the best way she could, the boys received a combined hug until the tears had subsided.

The boys had thought about what she'd said before drying their eyes with their hands and saying to her, 'Thanks, Miss.' They returned to the other children and the toys, smiles emerging from their little faces.

That afternoon, instead of eating her packed lunch in the office on her own, Ronny walked into the playground and sat next to Paula, one of the other workers there. Slightly surprised, Paula acknowledged her presence. 'Hi there. It's a lovely day today.'

'Yes, it is. I need to apologise to you all for being so aloof, so private and independent. I never intended to push you all away, but I realise now that I was doing just that. Next time you all go out for a curry outside working hours, I would love to be included.' A bit of a mouthful, but it had to be said.

'No problem. We're all going to Teignmouth after work next Wednesday; you're more than welcome to join us.' It was said sincerely by Paula, Ronny could tell.

'Thank you, I'd like to accept. I've just acquired a stepbrother who, as well as being a complete joker, has taught me some hard lessons in life.'

'Wow, that's so exciting. Tell me more!' Paula was interested and Ronny had wanted to confide in her. The whole dinner break had resulted in a tête a tête about both girls' lives in general. Returning to the children, Ronny had felt elated and attempted to sing some nursery rhymes to them, with her appalling musical voice. A giggle had emerged whilst singing, but the children knew no different, thankfully.

Back at the apartment that evening, with the scones all depleted, she rang her mother. Not a regular occurrence during the week, unless she'd wanted something or had a purpose to the call. There had been nothing brewing, except the weekend surprise which she'd been sworn to secrecy. It was completely out of character for Ronny.

Margaret had noted the change in her voice and asked if she was okay.

'Yes, I'm fine. Just wondering if I could pop over for a few hours. I'm feeling lonely and my scone rations have disappeared.'

'Of course, you can, Veronica, I mean, Ronny. As it happens, I've got a batch of cheese scones cooking in the oven now. You don't need an invitation, you know. Peter and I aren't spring chickens anymore.' Her mother had laughed at the thought of young love, replying as a mother should to her offspring.

'Thanks, Mum. I will be over soon.' With that, Ronny turned her television off, replaced her slippers with her shoes and walked slowly to the bakery shop flat. A couple had walked past her, holding hands. She'd recognised them and said hello, for which they'd acknowledged her presence. They'd both looked so loved up, enjoying each other's company. Ronny was so envious, she'd wanted that too, at some point in her life.

As she reached the flat, knocking on the front door before entering, she could hear a female voice in the kitchen, not her mother's. It was Lillian and she'd dropped off her evening's cooking for the next day's counter in the shop. The butterfly cakes looked too good to eat, the chocolate muffins delicious, and the carrot cake, a favourite of hers, divine. Ronny never appeared to put on weight whatever she'd ate, a bonus, but lately, her appetite was poor, no interest in food at all.

'Wow, it all looks scrumptious, Lillian,' Ronny had said to her. Asking after Michael, she was rewarded with a 'He's fine, Veronica.' Lillian obviously wasn't happy. Something was on her mind.

'Are you okay, Lillian?' Ronny asked, a little concerned.

'Actually, no, if you're asking. It's Martin, my oldest son. He and his girlfriend are separating, and he's packed his job in, a high powered one at that. He's taken a menial job here, locally. I'm not happy about it, all the studying he'd put into to get there.' She wasn't impressed at all.

'Look on the bright side; you'll see a lot more of him, won't you?' It was an observation, a positive one.

'Hardly, he will have the children to look after. She's moving away, so he will be the main parent.' She was a barrel of laughs, really down in the doldrums. 'His life is ruined, for sure.'

'Oh. I'm sorry, Lillian. All will work out, just give it time. Remember me to Michael and Mr Davies.' Ronny hadn't known what else to say, words had failed her.

Margaret reassured her that everything would turn out okay in the end, but she'd not convinced her, not really. As Lillian left to return to her husband, her mother shrugged her shoulders, causing an elevated laugh from Ronny.

'Mother! That wasn't called for.' The laughter followed again and Margaret joined in too.

Ronny had seldom seen the side of her she was seeing now, it was an eye-opener.

'These things happen, Veronica. It comes out in the wash, eventually. We managed without your father when he returned to Exeter to look after your grandfather, and he never came back. We coped okay. That's all history now.'

Ronny gasped without showing her mother. 'Where's Peter?' she said, changing the subject.

'In the bathroom, having a long soak. Just as well, after that pandemonium. Put the kettle on, I'm parched.' Margaret got on with the job at hand, her mind focused on the baking again.

More pastries, pies and biscuits were pulled out of the oven, cooling off on wire trays. Ronny espied small packets of Welsh cakes, miniature versions of the original. Small versions of coconut macaroons, too. Ronny smiled, her mother had listened to her, and she'd felt enlightened. She hugged her mother, thanking her. 'No, thank you,' had been the response.

As Ronny was about to leave for her apartment, loaded up with goodies, some still warm, Margaret stopped her.

'I forgot to mention it earlier. Your sister is coming down for the weekend, her and the twins. I'm booking the restaurant in Teignmouth for Saturday evening; I will add you to the number, okay?'

'Brilliant, I'm looking forward to it already.' Ronny replied, sounding excited. Walking back to her apartment, she realised that calls to Gina and Matt were urgently required. Tomorrow evening would have to suffice, as well as adding more bodies to the venue in Teignmouth. Life had suddenly become very busy.

Ronny's sleep pattern was more than disrupted that night. With so much going on in her mind, it had been no wonder. Lillian's reaction to her oldest son's dilemma was so out of context, and her mother's reaction was completely out of character, a bolt out of the blue for Ronny. Always the quiet body behind the bakery counter was Margaret's colleague and friend, her mother being the chatty one asking about any local gossip; their welfare coming first and foremost though, the main priority.

It had appeared strange that at home, Margaret hadn't divulged any information about anybody or anything, on neither a good nor a bad front. Her mother was a conversationalist when required to do so, but otherwise remained mainly reserved, solemn and subdued. Ronny suddenly saw herself as a copy of her, not having noticed the similarity in personality before. She was, indeed, a younger version of her mother.

Brilliant with the children in the nursery, but otherwise, a loner used to being on her own.

Getting on with life without interruption from others was paramount in her mind, most of the time. The remark concerning her father had her pondering for a long time. What had become of her grandfather? Was he still alive? If her father had initially set out to look after him during illness, maybe his death had contributed to him remaining in Exeter, his hometown, and never returning. Hopefully, Matt would have some answers there. She couldn't wait.

Gina was well excited at all the news Ronny had given her. She was looking forward to seeing Matt and Rose and welcoming the newcomers to the family. Always staying in the small bed and breakfast near her mother's flat, she wouldn't be anywhere in the vicinity of The Ness, and unlikely to bump into either of them until the restaurant meal organised in Teignmouth, well, almost organised!

Ronny updated her sister on life, in general, in the small village, nothing much to report really.

Mrs Parkinson had passed away at number 12, living next door to the bakery shop, a small quaint terraced house. Nothing had happened regarding the empty house, as yet. Her son and daughter were slowly sorting things out. Ronny remembered the loving grandmother and great grandmother, sat on the doorstep, happy enough people watching. Waving to known passers-by with a smile adorning her chiselled face. She was well into her 90s, a good age.

Gina returned the favour on her area of Scotland. Nothing much to report there either, Gina wasn't home a lot of the time, her career as a nurse taking up most of her time, outside looking after her five-year-old twins, that was. Alastair was there, working a nine-to-five office job, but kept the family life fairly private. Not one to meddle into neighbours' goings-on, unless specifically asked to do so. He was a football fanatic, the reason he wasn't joining the family in Shaldon, a ticket had been purchased to watch a match, live, his hobby outside family and work priorities.

She'd not mentioned Matt's jovial character; her sister could witness that for herself over the coming weekend. An outgoing personality, Gina would encourage him, she knew all too well. If Ronny had taken a shine to her stepbrother, Ronny was certain that Gina would, too.

'There is something I need to mention, Gina. I've started looking for Dad; it's time to reconnect with him if I can. Are you interested in meeting up with him again?' Ronny asked, very cautiously.

'Absolutely. He was a good father, as far as I can recall.'

'Good. I'm hoping Matt has some positive information about his whereabouts this weekend. He's doing some detective work for me. Peter, his dad and our dad were friends, a long time ago. Strange, but Mum opened up last night, telling me that Dad had returned to Exeter to look after Granddad, but never came back home. I wasn't aware of that, Gina,' Ronny responded. 'Were you?'

'No, I wasn't. Mum hid a lot of things from us in the early days. We never questioned her either. Perhaps we should have? The bakery took up most of her time, all of it if I'm honest. Thank heavens for Grandma being around to look after us.' Gina's answer had held food for thought.

'You're right. I'm looking forward to the weekend and seeing how much the twins have grown. Speak to you soon.' Ronny finished her call and hung up.

A cup of tea, something to eat and another two calls to make. One call to Matt and Rose, altering the initial plans of the last conversation, and after that, an additional count to the restaurant in Teignmouth. The cheese scones looked delicious, she'd decided. Buttering one and adding pickled onions, Branston pickle and jalapenos to her plate, Ronny devoured her meal before making the very urgent calls.

Matt had appeared enthusiastic about the get-together at the weekend. A meet up in Teignmouth was more than welcoming, an area new to him.

'All we want now is Mark to join us and we're almost there,' Matt had giggled loudly.

'Is he the identical twin brother I've heard about? God forbid he's got your personality, too! Your other brother's name doesn't happen to be Luke, by any chance?' Ronny was joking, the names of the Bible coming to mind immediately.

'Actually, it is. Luke lives in America now.' The comedian in Ronny hadn't registered at first.

Ronny's roar erupted before Matt had realised the joking remark made earlier.

'The *V*s in my family name have a competitor, Matt,' she was still laughing. 'Seriously though, is your mum still alive, just wondering? I'd love to meet her.'

'Yes and no,' he'd sounded so serious. 'Mum left us to join a religious sect, hence, our Christian names. I've no idea where she is now.'

'Really, I'm so sorry, Matt. I shouldn't have asked.' Ronny had felt awful for bringing up the subject.

'Gotcha, Sis.' The cackle from Matt had Ronny smelling a rat! 'Actually, Mum passed away two years ago. She was religious, I will admit, but as for our names, they hadn't come from the Bible.'

'I deserved that one. On a serious note, how is Rose? Are you looking after her?'

'Of course, I am. Ever the gentleman, me. Just to clear things up on the names' front, Matthew and Mark were Mum's uncles, twins at that. They both died in their teens, something genetic, I can't remember the medical term. Both my brother and I have been tested and neither of us has the condition in us. Luke was my grandfather's name; Lucas was his actual birth name, as is my brother's.' A little piece of family history to pass on.

'Well, thank you for that! I need my beauty sleep now. I will see you both soon. Bye for now.' Ronny quickly contacted the restaurant, adding two more guests to the group meal. Another blob of moisturising cream was definitely on the cards before going to sleep. Her sides had hurt, too.

Chapter Five

It was the twins' neighbour that had picked Ben and Aaron up on Friday. Their glum faces struggled to create a smile most of the day. Ronny had tried so hard to cheer them up, distractions hadn't worked though. It broke her heart seeing them like it. She'd spoken to them just before Mrs Turner had arrived to take them home.

'Are you both all right, boys?' she'd asked, knowing full well that they were far from it.

'Mummy has packed her suitcase to go to her new house. I don't want her to go,' Ben had offered, near to tears but holding his emotions in.

'Nor do I. I will miss her,' Aaron had volunteered.

Thankfully, they weren't crying. Ronny thought long and hard, wondering how to approach the situation.

'My daddy had to go and take care of my granddad when I was five years old, not much older than you two. He didn't come back, so my mummy had to look after my sister and me. I was sad to start off with too, but it was okay in the end.' The boys listened intently to what she was saying. 'You will see your mummy, but daddy will be there to put you to bed, and you will have Rufus to play with.' She'd so hoped that her words had helped.

'Okay, Miss,' they both said as Mrs Turner had walked into the nursery.

Ronny waved as they'd exited the building. She'd so wanted to take their pain away, but knew there was nothing she could do, nothing at all.

Rather than going straight to her apartment after work, Ronny had headed straight for the bakery shop. Her mother was packing everything up for the day, the cakes remaining placed in the refrigerator, to sell on the next day, not that there had been much left. The door was closed to customers, but Ronny tapped on the door and Peter opened it for her, closing it again afterwards.

'Hi, is everything okay?' he'd asked. 'You look a bit lost.'

'I've had an emotional day. I could do with some company. Is there anything I can do to help?'

'Yes, the floor requires a brush and a mop and the counter a wipe over, if you're willing,' Peter replied, not turning help down.

'I'm on the case. You both carry on with what you're doing.'

With everything done, a blank canvas again in preparation for the next day, Margaret locked the door behind them. 'You're welcome to have food with us, Ronny,' she was getting used to calling her by the unfamiliar name now. 'I've cooked a quiche and the salad is already prepared.' Margaret was holding the bowl of salad in her arms, extra to the day's requirement.

'Yes please, Mum.' Ronny headed the way to the flat.

After the meal was finished, followed by two cups of tea, some unexpected conversation between the three of them emerged. The weather, the fishermen, the busy day in the

56

shop, nothing overpowering at all. Ronny had enjoyed the few hours there. Getting up to leave for her apartment, she asked what time her mother had booked the restaurant for Saturday evening, the next day.

'Eight o'clock, from here please,' Margaret replied. 'Don't be late.'

Ronny had already known the answer, she'd added Matt and Rose to the group meal only a few days beforehand. Not wanting to spoil the surprise, Ronny had held up the pretence, knowing the outcome would be well worth it in the end.

Saturday was going to be a good day for the Johnson and the Sutherland clan (Peter's surname was Sutherland). It had been a pity that Ben and Aaron, the twins from the nursery, wouldn't be celebrating at their home over the weekend. Ronny walked back to the apartment, going directly to bed without even making her usual cup of tea. She loved those boys, as if they were her own, seeing them so upset was heart-wrenching.

Ronny woke up Saturday morning with a headache, a throbbing sensation that hadn't often occurred. She couldn't remember the last time she'd had one. Her almost sleepless night was probably a factor, she'd told herself. After a cold shower to hopefully help clear her head, a bowl of cereal and two cups of strong tea, Ronny had decided on a walk. She'd not engaged in her regular exercise for a long time.

Having so many other things going on, a new more-than-busy lifestyle erupting, the daily walks had stopped; she'd not found any time for them. With her comfortable trainers on, Sketchers the make, Ronny walked outside to clear her headache. Passing The Ness hotel, a decision to afford a large latte outside on the balcony after her walk, had entered her mind. She'd no idea what time Matt and Rose were checking in, and it had been no use waiting until they'd arrived from London; they would both be exhausted anyway, after the long drive. With Rose being pregnant, she would require rest before the group meal that evening.

Stopping outside the small café overlooking the harbour, checking out the marine memorabilia in the window, something she'd always done intermittently. There were new pieces of bric-à-brac to catch her eye; junk her mother would have called it, all waiting to be snapped up. A kitchen pegboard that was decorated with anchors and boats, with a space to put a small photograph in at the top. The board was big enough for lists and messages; Ronny had become forgetful of late, with everything going on and had decided to buy it.

Walking into the café, she pointed out the item to the assistant, searching for her purse in her jacket pocket, while the lady assistant sought it out for her.

'Miss, Miss,' she'd suddenly heard. Turning around Ben and Aaron were stood there beside her, smiling from ear to ear.

'Well, hello both, what are you doing here?' she asked them, so happy to see them with smiles on their little faces.

'Daddy has brought us for an ice cream in a glass,' they both replied in unison. 'Come and see him.' Ben had caught hold of her free hand, pulling her in the vicinity of the tables looking out over the gorgeous harbour views.

Indicating to the assistant to hold on, that she would be there in a minute, Ronny had had no option but to follow the twins. It had been Aaron that had spoken first.

'Miss, this is my daddy.' So excited he was.

'This is our dog, Rufus,' Ben had then said, not to be outdone by his brother.

The small black and white mongrel was sat obediently under the table, minding its own business, but had looked up on Ben's call. Ronny had to smooth it and acknowledge the little beast, it was obligatory. Its doleful eyes suddenly lit up at getting some attention from her.

'Martin Davies,' Ronny then shouted, much too loudly. 'Is that you?'

The twins' daddy then looked up, studied her carefully before saying, 'Veronica Johnson, well, well, well. Have a seat, please. Can I get you a coffee?'

'No, I will get one now. I was just buying something from the window. I will be back.' Ronny turned back to the counter, ordered a coffee and paid for the pegboard, as well as the beverage.

She couldn't believe he was the twins' father. They hadn't shared the same surname, and Lillian, her mother's friend and working colleague hadn't mentioned Martin having twins. Children, yes, but not twins. The connection had never arisen, and there had been no reason for it to have.

Carrying the coffee over, along with the bric-à-brac packaged in a small bag, she very nearly spilt the contents before reaching the table the twins and Martin had occupied.

'So, boys, how do you two know this lady then?' Martin had asked. 'I used to go to school with Veronica.'

'She's Miss,' replied Ben, all completely innocent.

'I work in the nursery they've attended since babies. I didn't realise you were their dad. It's always been their mother or Mrs Turner that pick them up in the afternoon.' She'd offered. 'And it's Ronny, not Veronica. Only my mother calls me that nowadays, oh and your mother when I see her.'

Martin informed her of his return to working in Teignmouth and taking over the responsibility of looking after the boys on a full-time basis. His partner, the boys' mother, had moved to Bristol and a new career opportunity. Ronny hadn't interrupted, after already hearing Lillian's side of the story, she'd wanted to hear Martin's.

'You're still together as a couple though?' Ronny had asked, afterwards.

'Unfortunately not, our relationship dwindled after the boys' birth, if I'm honest. My working away during the week didn't help, but the love between us had gone well before then.' It was quite a speech.

'I'm sorry, Martin, I really am.' Ronny's intuition about the boys' parents was indeed spot on all along. They'd not received the love outside the nursery that they'd deserved.

'Enough about me. Tell me, are you married, engaged, divorced? Children, animals, etc,' he'd asked, a snigger emerging afterwards.

'No, no, no, no and no. That's the short answer.' Ronny laughed, looking at him directly. Wow, he was handsome. Her skin was tingling. Martin had no resemblance to his brother at all, thankfully. Why she'd coloured, her face resembling a beetroot, she'd not been aware.

Martin had noticed though and laughed loudly. 'You always were a strange one, Veronica, I mean Ronny. Elusive, enigmatic, but with that certain something.'

'Well, thank you, I think!' Ronny picked her cup up awkwardly, her hand unsteady. Martin had noticed that, too.

'So, out of curiosity, what do you do for work, Martin?' Ronny had really wanted to know, all the details!

'Well, I was in highways and maintenance, based in London, in the offices. IT really, all a bit boring but it paid well, very well indeed. I start a new job here on Monday, in Teignmouth harbour. Still office-based primarily, ensuring all is shipshape and in Bristol fashion there, paperwork-wise, that is. Ha, ha, that was a good joke, even if I say so myself.' Martin stopped momentarily, before continuing. 'Money isn't everything, Ronny. It's taken me a long time to realise it, my mother isn't happy about my change of career either, but I'm here to stay, with my boys as company.' Rufus popped his head up from under the table. 'Not forgetting the dog,' he added, smiling.

'I've never had any to worry about on that score, but I'd agree wholeheartedly. I'm happy here, wouldn't want to be anywhere else.' Finishing her coffee, Ronny got up from the chair. 'Well, I've got to go. We've got a group meal tonight in Teignmouth: my sister, her twins, and my stepbrother and his partner, to name a few. Thanks for the company; I will see you boys soon.'

Martin stopped her. 'All sounds interesting; I'd love to know more. Same time, same place, next Saturday?' He waited for a response.

'You're on. I will see you all then.' She walked out of the door, not knowing quite what had happened there!

The large latte at The Ness had had to wait. Walking back to her apartment, Ronny's day was now completely out of sync. Her belly rumbled, she'd needed food, a light lunch, a soak in the bath in preparation for the meal that evening, and decisions as to what to wear. Not one to dress up, Gina was the opposite, and Rose was an unknown entity. Jeans and a tidy top just wouldn't do.

Hunting through her wardrobe, an elegant turquoise blouse with a tied front and black trousers were pulled out for perusal. Both required ironing, creased because of the number of clothes crammed tightly into the limited space. Would they still fit, though? The outfit hadn't been worn in ages, so long ago her memory couldn't envisage the occasion at all. She'd decided to prepare a sandwich and a cup of tea first, before trying the garments on.

Settled on the settee, eating her sandwich, a huge smile beamed across her face. Martin Davies had always attracted the girls at school. The high school heartthrob: he'd loved the attention and revelled in it. Probably going out with every available schoolgirl in his class, Ronny was in the class below and two years his junior. Gina had had a short fling with him, but it hadn't lasted. He'd lost no sleep over the breakups, moving onto other available beauties, breaking everyone's hearts.

Unlike his brother, Michael, his intellect commanded a stint in college, followed by university in Bristol. Ronny had lost touch of his movements after that but hadn't really shown any interest anyway. She'd not wanted to follow in the other girls' footsteps, being used for his sexual prowess, but was always aware of how handsome he was. Now she was drooling over his good looks and had agreed to meet him in the café in a week's time. Was that wise?

They weren't teenagers anymore, her argument within herself. He was 32 years old and she was 30. Surely, the old Martin wasn't still around. With two delightful and thoroughly captivating twin boys, he'd grown up, he must have! Like it or not, Ronny was going to keep the invitation; she wouldn't know otherwise, would she?

Thankfully, the clothes had still fitted. She'd felt uncomfortable, but was prepared to make the effort, this once. The ironing board was retrieved from the cupboard, the iron plugged in and the outfit hung up devoid of creases. Now time for a soak in the bath, time to relax for a while. The radio played from the main lounge area, and Ronny heard Elvis Presley singing again. Her favourite song of all time, *It's Now or Never*. Was that an omen, she'd thought to herself.

As Ronny arrived at her mother's flat, she'd received a text from Matt and Gina, both saying they were there at the restaurant, ready and waiting, and that they had all become acquainted with one another. Gina had added that Matt was quite a character, something that had already been apparent to her. She smiled reading it.

Margaret and Peter were both patiently waiting as she'd entered the flat. She was grateful for her mother being dressed in her best togs, as she'd now known that she wouldn't feel out of place herself.

'You look nice, Ronny,' her mother remarked.

'So do you, Mum,' Ronny had replied.

As they'd seated themselves in the taxi, Peter at the front with the driver and the ladies at the back, Margaret had asked how her day had gone, so far. Not wanting to disclose the meeting with Martin, she'd not lied. Telling her mother that the twins from the nursery and their father had met up by accident and that they'd enjoyed a coffee in the café. It was the truth.

'I was going for a walk; my head was banging. I can't remember the last time I had a headache.' It was all true.

'It's nice for you to meet up with people, Ronny (the more affectionate name now appeared to trip off her tongue). Cooped up in that apartment all the time wasn't doing you any favours.' Margaret had spoken meaningfully.

'I know. I'm going out with my work colleagues next week for a curry in Teignmouth. I'm looking forward to it.' Ronny had meant it.

The taxi pulled up outside the restaurant and they all got out, Peter paying the usual fare and telling the driver what time to pick them up for the return journey. The twins, Gina's children, were first to run to Ronny, having changed completely since she'd last seen them. Jenny's hair had grown so much; she was now a beautiful princess. Blond locks halfway down her back with a trail of natural ringlets at the end. A gorgeous little girl.

Jonathan had shot up, height-wise, towering well above Jenny and looking similar to a mini Alastair. They'd not looked like twins at all. Comparing them to Ben and Aaron, who had both resembled one another, although Ronny had easily differentiated between them; their height and weight were identical and their hair colour was pure blond.

'I've missed you both,' she'd said to them.

'We've missed you as well, Aunty Ronny.' They were adorable.

Matt had walked out of the restaurant, picking up Jonathan and play fighting with him, all in good fun. Jonathan was laughing noisily as Matt had almost tickled him to death.

'Matthew! What are you doing here?' Peter then asked, completely surprised.

'We've got something to tell you, Dad. All will be revealed after the meal.' It had sounded mysterious.

As they walked into the restaurant and espied Matt's fiancé, Peter's face had lit up. He was mesmerised at first, before hugging Rose and welcoming her to the meal and to sunny Teignmouth. It was sunny that day.

Gina had no problems communicating with the others, neither had Ronny, come to that. Their mother was happy and it had shown all over her face. Seated next to her, she'd whispered to Ronny.

'Did you know about this all along? Matt and Rose joining us, I mean.'

'Of course, I did. Matt tells me everything, well almost!' had been the reply. A giggle had erupted, so she placed a hand across her mouth to hide it, before being reprimanded by her mother.

'I'm so glad you get on so well. I was a little worried that you wouldn't.'

'Everything's fine, Mum. Relax and enjoy yourself.' Ronny turned to Rose, getting to know her better, a lovely conversation; she had really liked Matt's fiancé.

With the meal finished, Matt stood up from his chair, looking over his entire family and smiling. A smile as big as a Cheshire cat.

'Well, I'm pleased to announce that Rose and I are going to have a baby, well, Rose is giving birth to it, not me!' Ever the joker, Matt couldn't be serious for a moment. 'So, Jenny and Jonathan are going to have a cousin to play with. I think it's only one,' looking towards Rose, who had nodded positively, he wiped his brow playing the fool, again.

The applause had everyone in the restaurant looking up, wondering what was going on. After the clapping had stopped, Margaret then said, 'What about the wedding first?'

Children came after marriage as far as she was concerned. A stickler to tradition was Ronny and Gina's mother.

'Give me a chance!' Margaret had caught him on the hop.

Rose's look was one of surprise; they'd been engaged for over two years now. 'Well, it's news to me, but I'm all for arranging a small wedding before the baby arrives.'

Another applause from the family had created the same result. Onlookers were wondering what the joyful occasion was all about. From the top of his voice, Matt uttered, for all to hear.

'We're getting married and having a baby, folks.' The happiness was apparent in his voice.

Everyone in the restaurant stood up, applauding them. The atmosphere was euphoric, emotions full to brimming, in awe of the happy occasion. Peter and Margaret's expressions were one of pure joy, exhilaration and both full of life, all of a sudden. The "oldies" were elated, showing their true colours in all their glory, at long last. Revelling in the family there today, others still absent, but for now, a true reason to celebrate.

Chapter Six

Matt and Rose had arranged for Ronny to join her at The Ness for Sunday lunch, with the hotel's approval, of course. They were staying another day and night before heading back to London on Monday. Time to visit Peter and Margaret at the flat and show Rose around the area. As small as Shaldon was, combined with Teignmouth, there was plenty to see and explore.

Ronny had arranged to meet up with her sister, Gina, in the afternoon, after lunch; there was a small communal park nearby to keep the children busy, allowing the sisters to sit on one of the benches and talk, she'd hoped. It would be nice to catch up face to face, on a sibling-to-sibling level. The meal, the evening before, had gone without any issues. Everyone had enjoyed the few hours spent together, her mother especially. Ronny recalled the evening as she'd dressed for lunch with Matt and Rose. The black trousers had been worn again but with a different top, a floral affair which she'd usually worn with her jeans.

As she walked the short journey to the hotel, Matt was there to meet her. Rose had already made herself comfortable on one of the tables overlooking the fabulous view. A wave from her indicated where she was. Ronny couldn't quite believe she was having lunch at The Ness; she pinched herself to check if it was all real.

The waiter scribbled their drinks order onto a small notepad, along with three beef roast dinners for their main meal. All had refused a starter course. Rose was looking tired, so Ronny asked her if she was okay.

'Yes, I'm fine, thank you. Getting up early on a Sunday morning isn't usual for me, my one day of rest throughout the week. At these prices, I wasn't about to miss out on the breakfast,' Rose had replied. 'Late mornings will soon be a thing of the past for both of us,' she'd added, rubbing her belly. The baby would more than keep her busy.

One after her own heart, Ronny had thought. Her chances of ever staying there at the hotel were slim, but any paid meals would not be missed, not in a million years. Rose had commented on the views from the balcony with extreme excitement, so breath-taking, an experience she would never have discovered in London.

'You are lucky living here, Ronny. I'm not sure if I could live here permanently, but never say never,' she said rubbing her belly again. Who knew? The little baby yet to be born could change her outlook on things for the future completely.

The waiter arrived with the coffees and a large beer, and talk between the three of them begun, prior to the Sunday lunch being served. Ronny had filled Matt in on her findings regarding her father's whereabouts. More so, her mother's brief comments of late. Now it was Matt's turn.

'Your dad is still living in the house he was born in, Ronny,' he'd offered.

'What! He's at my grandparents' house in Exeter,' she shouted at first, before remembering where she was, then spoke softly for the duration of her visit.

'Yes, he's a carer for your grandmother. She's got onset dementia, has had it for a few years now. Your grandfather passed away a long time ago, I'm afraid.' The facts had been revealed.

Somehow, the fact that her grandfather wasn't still around hadn't surprised her at all. From her mother's remarks about her dad returning to Exeter to care for him during illness, it had seemed only logical. Why he hadn't returned home after his death though, was another story needing clarification.

Apparently, her father had asked her mother, Margaret, to move back to Exeter after her grandfather's death. He'd not felt comfortable leaving his mother on her own. Margaret had refused to leave Shaldon after struggling with life there beforehand. The relationship had broken up as a result: Matt's findings on the relationship so far.

'That still doesn't explain why Dad had started sending us birthday cards as children, before stopping altogether without reason. Is he in another relationship, Matt?' Ronny had asked.

'No, there's only ever been Margaret. His life has revolved around his parents' welfare and work. Maybe, they were paramount in keeping you and your sister at a distance. I've got the address, Ronny. It's up to you what you want to do with it.' Matt had handed her a piece of paper with an address on it and she took it from him.

'Thank you, Matt. I have to mull things over on that score, and talk to Mum first.' Things were going to be tricky. 'I'm truly grateful for this.' Ronny glanced at the piece of paper before placing it in her purse safely.

Conversation reverted to the baby and the wedding. Rose had something in mind, but being very short notice, confirmation on certain matters had required checking up on. She'd not minded a quiet affair, preferred it, in fact. 'All will be revealed,' she'd said, causing intrigue in Matt's eyes.

Pretending to be scared, he chewed at his fingernails, before receiving a tap on the knuckle from Rose. 'Give it a break,' she'd said annoyingly.

With general conversation continuing, Rose had disclosed that she'd been born and raised in Cornwall before moving to London as a child. So, she had lived on the coast at some point in her life. The unshed tears in her eyes realised a past she'd remembered, happy times. Ronny comforted her with a hug. Her parents were now divorced but had remained in London, now in different relationships. She was still close to them both.

With the food now in front of them, the table became quiet, all concentrating on the task at hand; eating the delicious meal, and it was absolutely delicious. Three empty plates had confirmed that. With enough room in their stomachs for a dessert, coffee and mints as a finale, all were satisfied. Ronny had taken her purse from her bag to pay for her portion of the bill, but Matt wouldn't hear of it.

'Put your money away, Sis. This is on us. Spend it on your boyfriend.' Matt had noticed a difference in her. 'Something has happened, Ronny. Pray tell your big brother!' The clown had re-emerged.

Ronny confided in them both about Martin and the twins, leaving out the fact that he was Lillian's son. They were both sworn to secrecy until Ronny could decide whether he was still the schoolboy Casanova, and to be trusted. Happy faces had wished her the best, Ronny promising to keep in touch with anything that was relevant.

The invitation to their wedding was mandatory, no was not an answer, not acceptable at all.

The formalities would be announced soon, very soon. Margaret was blamed for the rush, but smiles adorned their faces, she'd merely pushed the button forward, because of values of tradition. The future was about to become very busy, a wedding, a birth and deciding on plans regarding her father. If she'd not had a headache now, there would definitely be one looming in the not-too-distant future.

Saying goodbye, Ronny headed for the small park to meet Gina and the twins, and yet another tête-à-tête about anything and everything. What had happened to her quiet, uncluttered lifestyle?

She'd only now realised what living was all about, the hard way!

Jenny had seen her coming towards the park and ran towards her. Jonathan was climbing up the steps of the slider, preparing to slide down on his stomach, rather than his bottom. *Children will be children*, she'd thought to herself, smiling.

'Hi, Aunty Ronny. How are you today?' she asked her.

'I'm very well, thank you. Are you both enjoying yourselves?' Ronny asked.

'Yes. Mummy is over there.' Pointing to one of the seats near the older children's swings, Ronny headed that way as Jenny followed her brother on the slider.

'Hi, Sis. Have you recovered after last night? Overall, things went well, I thought. I've just had lunch with Matt and

71

Rose; I love them both to bits.' It was the truth: they were lovely people.

'They are brilliant company, Matt being the joker of the pack. So, what's new?' There was no beating about the bush where Gina was concerned.

Ronny filled her in on all she knew, Matt's findings, their mother's little comments about the past, and the wedding between Rose and Matt.

'Trust Mum to insist on a wedding before the baby's arrival. They've got their work cut out there. Keep me updated, Sis,' Gina had said.

'I need to interrogate Mum before approaching Dad. She's hiding something, I'm sure. Somehow, I don't think Dad is entirely to blame regarding their break-up. It's a sneaking suspicion, and I could be wrong, but I'm not as a rule.' Ronny had convinced herself.

'I'm inclined to believe it was a joint decision, but you're welcome to beaver away at your heart's content. Don't let me stop you.' Gina had turned towards the area the twins were playing in. 'Kids, come back here, where I can see you, please.'

Gina was a good mother, a little stern at times, but a cuddly mum all said and done. The twins adored her. Margaret had never been that type of mother to Ronny and Gina, though she'd loved them, all the same. Their Shaldon grandmother, Nanny Joyce, had held them close, sneaked the odd chocolate bar to them when Margaret wasn't looking and laughed with them often. The prim and proper Margaret had shown a different side to her the evening before though, and it was strange seeing her with her hair down, so to speak. Good too, no complaints.

There was more to their parents' break up than they'd already dug up, and Ronny was determined to prise it out of her mother, no matter how long it took. Ronny's soul went out to her father, not seeing his little girls grow up to become the people they were today. Was it purely a break-up due to locations? Gina had no answer either way; their regular conversations over the phone were more about the twins than anything else. A grandmother's prerogative.

Gina was going back to Scotland on Monday. She'd already paid a visit to Margaret and Peter at their flat. Ronny had asked whether they'd wanted to go back to her apartment from the park for a few hours.

'No, I'm taking the children for a walk across the bridge to Teignmouth, past the newly built roundhouse and up the main shopping area. A stop in a café and an ice cream for the children, you're welcome to join me.' Gina had offered.

'Okay, I'd love to. The weather isn't too cold and the sun is shining, all good on the western front, as they say!' She was beaming from ear to ear.

'What's with you? You've changed Ronny and for the better, I might add.' It was more of a statement really. 'Come on then, kids, who's up for a walk and an ice cream?' Neither adult had required an answer; the response was an obvious yes.

Not a usual route for Ronny, the twins had stopped to admire the roundhouse along the way, a delightful home, shaped like a curvy seashell. The owners had built the home at the bottom of the garden of their existing family home, overlooking the sea. It was a sight to behold, modern, chic, but classy. The new build was shown on *Grand Designs* television programme, Channel 4, combined spiral staircases and curves on all levels. Plenty of glass, loads, in fact, all quite unique. Ronny had still preferred the quaint terraced cottages on one of Shaldon's normal streets if given the choice. An old girl in a young(ish) body was Ronny. Anything modern was ruined on her.

The walk was a mixture of a flat road, inclining in several places, but not a steep gradient. The twins' little legs had required a rest, so stopping off in the newsagents, cum grocery shop, cum souvenir shop, Ronny had treated them to an ice cream, their choice. Their little eyes lit up and their minds pondered for ages, deciding which one to choose. Finally, with the lollies in their mouths, they all walked towards the Teignmouth seafront and a small café-cum-amusement arcade, all rolled into one.

Ronny resisted the two pence tipping point game, her favourite, heading directly towards a vacant table at the other end of the arcade. It had been Gina that had ordered the coffees and paid for them, Ronny ensuring the children were seated correctly on the plastic seats around the good-sized plastic table. Looking out onto the front, she'd espied Matt and had called out to him loudly. He hadn't turned around on her call, so standing up and moving slowly towards the pavement, she shouted again. 'Matthew, over here!'

As he'd turned around, she'd thought she'd seen a ghost. It wasn't Matt, the dress sense was all wrong, after seeing him at The Ness not many hours earlier. He approached her, though, realising that Ronny was shouting at him.

'I'm sorry. I thought you were someone else.' The man standing beside her was almost identical, astoundingly so: his height, weight, hairstyle and colour, and his eyes equally hypnotic. The voice wasn't right, or the personality (first

74

impression). A light-bulb moment had suddenly hit her and she'd uttered, 'Your name doesn't happen to be Mark, does it?'

'Yes, it does. I don't know you, do I?' he'd said very seriously.

'No, but I know your twin brother Matt, and your father, Peter. I am right, aren't I?' Ronny looked at him directly. She was convinced, 100%.

Gina then added to the conversation, agreeing wholeheartedly with her sister. 'Have a seat, Mark,' she said. 'Can I get you a coffee?'

With a meeting up of family in mind, Ronny phoned her stepbrother. As he'd picked up the call, she'd asked him where he was at that precise moment in time. He was actually minutes away from their destination, window shopping, of sorts.

'I will get two coffees in; I'm in the amusement arcade's café. There's someone here I'd like you to meet. Gina and the twins are with me. You can't miss us.'

'What are you up to now, Sis? Okay, we're almost there, Rose needs a rest as it happens.' Matt had rung off.

Mark did as he'd been told, sat on one of the vacant seats with the others, leaving Ronny to organise the beverages. Nothing much happened, the twins ogling him, really confused. Jonathan wasn't getting his tickles, or playtime, but said nothing. Gina, being Gina, had decided to let Ronny deal with the surprise at hand.

As Matt walked up to the café entrance, his shriek was deafening. 'Mark, what are you doing here?'

The shock could have killed him. 'What are you doing here?' The words were identical.

75

Rose pulled up another seat and laughed. 'Well, I never. It's about time you two aired your differences. Now is a perfect time.' Her remarks had put Ronny in an awkward position, not knowing they'd had words. She blushed initially, turning to avoid the confrontation.

'Well, this is nice, isn't it? I'm Ronny, your stepsister, by the way. This is Gina, also your stepsister, and Jenny and Jonathan, her twins.' It was a fact.

'Pleased to meet you all,' Mark had uttered. What could he say, in all honesty?

All drinking their coffees, the atmosphere froze momentarily. Rose was the one to break the cold chill with 'I'm pregnant, Mark. You're going to be an uncle. I'm organising a wedding too, in the not-too-distant future. It's so nice to see you again.' She'd meant it, most sincerely.

Mark did congratulate her, almost immediately. He'd had no quarrel with Rose, and liked her as a person, always had. She'd gotten caught up in the middle of it all, through no fault of her own. The solemn look adorning his face was suddenly tinged with a few happy lines, a smile breaking out. It had been a start, any roads.

Chapter Seven

With their coffees depleted, the ladies and the children headed for the amusements, a nose around the machines and Ronny's guilty pleasure, the two pence tipping point machine. An apt reason to leave the men to talk among themselves, whilst trying to win a soft toy from one of the numerous grabber machines there. No luck this time, the children were so disappointed.

Hopefully, the men were airing their grievances and sorting things out. With enough time allowed, returning to the table, there had been no blood baths as far as they could see. A good sign, Ronny had her fingers crossed behind her back. Going by their facial expressions, nothing sinister had occurred either. Siblings were prone to differences, nothing unusual there.

Rose had spoken first, saving the moment. 'Matt, we do have to see your dad before we go back to London tomorrow. There's no time like the present. Are you joining us, Mark?'

Time had stood still before Mark replied, 'Why not? Head the way; I've no idea where he lives.'

Ronny's fingers were still crossed. Gina's silence suddenly resulted in a gasp. She'd held her breath in for dear life, awaiting the response. The twins were fidgeting now, requiring activity. It was time to disband the group and all head separate ways.

Rose said her goodbyes to Ronny and Gina, gave the twins a hug before putting a £10 note in each of their hands. 'Thank you,' they'd both replied with huge smiles adorning their little faces. Turning to the men, she beckoned them to follow her and they obediently conformed. A hand gesture, telling Ronny that she would ring her soon, had her feeling relieved.

Walking back the way they'd come; Gina's bed and breakfast was now in view. It was time for Ronny to say goodbye to her and the twins, until next time.

'Have a safe journey back tomorrow and say hello to your daddy for me,' she'd said to the twins. 'Thanks for today, Gina. I will keep you updated.' The emotions were beginning to get the better of her now.

'You had better. I'm not sure what is going on here, but Shaldon and Teignmouth are busier than Edinburgh, if that's possible, on the personal family issues level that is. What, or who is going to turn up next?' Gina's giggles were infectious, causing Ronny to join in. Thankfully, her sister hadn't an incline about Martin Davies being back in the area. As an ex-boyfriend of hers, she could only envisage her feelings regarding him as a person, and nothing positive had sprung to mind.

Walking back to her apartment alone, Ronny had thought long and hard about the day she'd had. She couldn't have written it if she'd tried. Why Mark was here? Where he was staying, and how long he'd been in the area? All questions requiring answers, sooner rather than later. Her head had begun to hurt; a long soak in the bath, a cup of strong tea and two paracetamol tablets had all sounded heavenly. The first song on the radio had just happened to be Elvis Presley's *You're the Devil in Disguise*, how ironic was that!

Monday had returned to normality; Ronny had sighed relief. Not sure how much more her little brain could take; the highlight of her morning was Martin bringing the boys to the nursery. She'd tried to remain cool and aloof as he'd walked up to her, but her nerves had got the better of her. Of course, he'd noticed, his grin had confirmed it. What was the matter with her? She was behaving like a frightened child.

'Hello, Miss,' the boys had said excitedly.

'Hello to you both. There's Lego over there, your favourite. Can I have an aeroplane please?' she'd said to them. Ben and Aaron had both required a goal, so asking for something specific always worked. Charlie, the little boy they played with most of the time was of a very similar nature. Ronny's link with the children in her care was second to none.

The twins ran over to where Charlie was making what had looked like a car, joining in and searching for pieces to replicate an aeroplane. Their concentration on the subject was so enthralling. Ronny had laughed to herself, forgetting that Martin was stood by her side.

'I hope your weekend went well, Ronny. The boys couldn't stop talking about you after you'd left on Saturday.' Martin had commented. 'All good, mind.'

'Your boys are a treasure, Martin. I don't have favourites in the nursery (she'd lied) but Ben and Aaron would be mine if I did. They are adorable. Yes, Saturday evening and Sunday all went well. To be fair, I'm exhausted now. Back to little old me again and peace and quiet.' No truer words had Ronny spoken.

'I was wondering whether we could catch up before Saturday morning. I could get Mrs Turner to babysit. You name the venue.'

Ronny hadn't expected that at all. She could feel herself colouring up again, turning to look at the children in the nursery to avoid Martin seeing it. 'I really want to call in at Mum's after work tonight for an hour or two. Wednesday I'm out with the work colleagues for a curry. I'm free tomorrow if that's okay. Fish and chips would suit me perfectly.' What was she getting herself into?

'A cheap date, then. I'm all for that! Can you meet me outside the café? We can walk into Teignmouth, there's a nice chippie there I'm partial to.' Martin smiled at her, waiting for a response.

'Absolutely. Eight o'clock, is that okay?' She'd required a change of clothing first.

'Perfect. I'm looking forward to it already. I will see you later to pick up the little rascals.' He hadn't meant it; well, Ronny had hoped he hadn't.

She hadn't meant it when she'd told Martin she was calling in to see her mother, not at the time, but it was becoming a good idea. Margaret and Peter could fill her in on Matt and Mark's visit, curious as to how things had gone. With no one knowing that Mark was in the locality at the time, the surprise was on everyone.

Margaret must have been psychic. She'd rang on her lunchbreak, wanting her to call around after work. 'I will prepare an evening meal,' she'd offered.

'No problem, Mum. I had decided to come around anyway. Food would be great, thanks.'

The day had flown by, so much to do at work and so much on her mind. Her head was spinning, but she'd not had a headache. Grateful that one of the other working colleagues had attended to the twins' father when he'd picked them up, Ronny had sighed relief. She'd not avoided him purposely but was busy attending to something else in the nursery at the time.

With everything put away, all preparations in place for the children the next day, a short walk to the bakery shop should clear her head, temporarily. Ronny had been summoned by her mother; what for, she'd had no clue. A telling off, she'd guessed, not knowing what for really, though.

Remembering Nanny Joyce, when she was alive, one look from her had told the story. A reprimand was in order for something or other. 'Veronica, come here please,' she would command, knowing full well what the telling off was about. Ronny was a naughty child, as she'd recalled, no excuses.

The shop was almost sorted when she'd approached the shop, Peter having brushed the floor, mopped and wiped the counter over. A bag of food to take up to the flat sat on the counter, and all surplus sweet fancies were stored in the refrigerator overnight. Margaret had looked stressed, noticeably so.

'Are you okay, Mum? You look worn out.' It had been true. Her aged wrinkles were protruding.

'I'm a little preoccupied with things at present, but otherwise, I'm okay, thank you.' That had sounded ominous.

As they locked the shop door and headed up the stairs to the flat, Peter immediately put the kettle on to boil, gagging for a cup of tea.

'That was a hectic day. I think it's an early night for me.' A placid gentleman, Peter was never a big conversationalist at the best of times.

A salad bowl, pork pies and potato salad were placed on the dining table. Buttered bread rolls put on a large plate and Margaret's delicious apple turnovers for dessert. The brewed tea was ready, and they all seated around the table eating their meal. There was an eerie silence, waiting for someone to speak. Peter had started the conversation.

'Well, that was a surprise yesterday afternoon, Ronny. A bolt out of the blue, to be honest.' he'd said, waiting for a response.

'Mark, we are talking about, I presume,' Ronny responded. 'Matt and Rose's attendance on Saturday was an equally lovely surprise for you both. A grandchild and a wedding. You must be a proud father.'

'Absolutely, on the Matthew score, but Mark I was referring to. He'd only checked into the bed and breakfast in Teignmouth 30 minutes before you'd all met. He hadn't told me he was coming. He's looking for property to lease for his restaurant, and there's one he's viewed today.' Peter had put her in the picture.

'That's good. I hope it's what he's looking for,' Ronny replied. Looking at her mother, who was quietly eating her food, pushing food across her plate, she spoke again. 'Mum, what's up?'

'I will speak to you later, Ronny. Thanks to you and Rose, the boys are talking again. I appreciate that, I really do.' Margaret's acknowledgement was welcomed, but what else did she have to say?

'Rose is sorting out the wedding venue as we speak, and Mark has agreed to be the best man, reluctantly at first. I'm in touch with Luke, hoping to get all my boys together.' Peter was feeling elated, his expression proving it.

'I'm so pleased for you, Peter. Hopefully, I can get to know Mark better. Is he staying long?' Ronny was interested.

'Yes, he's here for the week, well until Saturday. There is more than one property he wants to see, but today's is his favourite and most reasonable, pricewise that is. I've given him your phone number; I hope you don't mind. He wants to meet up with you while he's here.'

'No problem, Peter. I'm looking forward to it.' Was she really?

With the meal finished, Peter took the empty plates into the kitchen. She could hear the kettle on to boil again, the noise filtering into the lounge/dining area. Margaret fussed about with the uneaten bread rolls and remaining salad in the bowl. She wasn't entirely with it, subdued and in a world of her own.

'Mum. What's wrong? Please tell me.' Ronny was begging now.

'I've got cooking to do later tonight, but we have to talk privately, soon. When are you free, if I can bake a double lot of cakes, pastries and quiches the evening before? A meal in the local public house, just the two of us, if that's okay for you.'

'I'm out tomorrow evening and Wednesday evening, Mum. What about Thursday, I've nothing planned for the evening then,' Ronny was concerned, her mother was being very mysterious.

Margaret had agreed. She'd looked lost and bewildered. Was she ill?

A further cup of tea and a conversation with Peter whilst Margaret had started cooking in the kitchen. Ronny wanted to question her stepfather on her mother's mood but kept her mouth firmly shut. Knowing her, she would only make matters worse, Calamity-Jane style. She had been so lucky that all had ended well with Matt and Mark, such a relief. Ronny's ability to put her foot in it had held no bounds, and not purposely done either. She was an accident waiting to happen, probably the reason she had kept herself to herself for so long.

Saying her goodbyes, she left for home, taking the salad bowl remains with her, an insistence from her mother. It will only go to waste, she'd stated, better she'd ate it. Ronny hadn't argued with her. Arranging to meet up at the local public house on Thursday after work, a hug was reciprocated before climbing down the stairs and walking slowly home to her apartment.

A long soak in the bath, Ronny's answer to everything. It had helped her relax, aided her sleep, and along with the music wafting in from the main living area, was very therapeutic. With an Elvis Presley DVD playing, a bubblicious bath (Ronny's name for a bubble bath) was enjoyed. Relaxing for absolute ages, the song *Memories* played, bringing thoughts of her father when she was very young. Good thoughts, at that.

Playing in the local park in Shaldon, and the much bigger version when living in Exeter, Vernon, her dad, had loved spending time with her and her sister. She could see the smile on his face even now, over two decades later. Margaret, her mother, would be home cooking and cleaning, leaving the girls' dad time alone. He'd never wondered why she wouldn't join them, her excuses always due to keeping the house up together and preparing food for their ever-hungry bellies.

Vernon had trusted everybody, often to his own detriment. Shrugging issues off as nothing when working, believing all that was said, he'd minded his own business and got on with his work. If somebody had told him that black was white, he would have believed that, too. Ronny had suddenly remembered the conversation he'd had with the girls, as he headed back to Exeter to help look after his father, their grandfather. A memory coming to light after all these years.

His promises of returning as soon as he could hadn't evolved, the promise had been broken.

Vernon never returned, and to this day, neither she nor Gina had had any contact with him. Matt had given her his address, her grandparents' house; he'd been there all along. The memories of yesterday couldn't be taken away, the good old days. Margaret's familiar words often remembered, usually in jest, but today it had relevance about it. At such a tender age playing with her dad, they were the good old days. Good memories, good fun, a good family connection, once, a long time ago.

The tears fell then, dampening the bubbles, turning them to water. She couldn't stop them, and let them fall into the bathwater, regardless. Maybe, with all that had gone recently, the outburst was just what was required. Leaving room for whatever her mother had to say on Thursday, Ronny was well in the dark there. No clues whatsoever, she'd honestly expected a telling off. How naïve could she be?

Elvis continued to play; Ronny had attempted to sing along, disastrously. Almost falling asleep in the bath, often a regular occurrence in her apartment, Ronny got out. The water was freezing, her skin now crinkled with the length of time laid there, thinking. Her pyjamas were ready to put on, warmed on the electric towel rail. A quick dry of her shoulder-length hair, ten minutes maximum, and she was ready to call it a night.

The DVD was coming to an end, the final song starting to play. It was a memorable song with more than significant words, *Don't!* Had Elvis's music been trying to tell her something? Turning the album off, a cup of milky coffee was prepared, the front and back door locked, and all and everything shut to the world for the rest of the night. There was a new day tomorrow. 'Oh,' she'd said to herself, remembering.

Meeting up with Martin for fish and chips, no less; her choice, admittedly. After all the goings-on tonight with her mother and stepfather, her concerns were whether he would, indeed, turn out to still be the schoolgirl Casanova of the past. Had he changed, for the better? Another discovery in the pipeline. For Ben and Aaron's sake, Ronny had hoped Martin had become the faithful partner as he'd gotten older, even with working away for a career.

Margaret hadn't asked where she was going tomorrow, she'd been thankful. A little white lie would have resulted until the elusive father of the twins she adored had shown his true colours. Tomorrow was looking like an equally difficult day, from start to finish. Time for sleep, she'd decided.

Chapter Eight

Ronny had a shower early the next morning in preparation for work at the nursery. She'd tossed and turned all night, throwing the bedclothes on and off intermittently, as she'd become hot and cold throughout the hours trying to sleep. Eventually, after giving up, a cup of tea was made and the radio was put on to listen to music. It wasn't going to happen, so what was the point!

A change from Elvis, she had listened to a channel mainly playing country and western songs. Elvis's single *Don't* had remained in her head from the night before, prominently so. The words had played on her mind.

Don't, Don't, that's what you say
Each time that I hold you this way
When I feel like this and I want to kiss you
Baby, don't say don't
Don't, don't, don't, don't

Ronny had shivered, though not because she was cold. She'd so wanted Martin to kiss her, a lasting intimate connection to seal their relationship; but the reservations were there, the constant niggling doubts. Would she want to leave his embrace, from being enveloped in his warm arms? That was where Ronny had so wanted to be right now. It had felt so right all of a sudden, a dream in the making. Ronny was fixated before they'd even begun to discover each other properly.

When the night grows cold, held in Martin's arms had sounded perfection in itself; everything she'd ever hoped for in a joint commitment. Settled on the sofa watching a film on the television, bodies entwined in a completely relaxed state of contentment. It had sounded so heavenly. Was it reachable, though, for a nobody like Ronny? What was so special about Veronica Johnson? Nothing had sprung to mind, nothing convincing anyway.

So, was Martin playing a game? Reconstructing his high school days, on a mission to break Ronny's heart. She sighed a deep sigh before shaking her head nervously. Could she trust him now the years had passed and Martin was no longer a teenager? He was still a heartthrob and a definite head-turner, even now. Ronny shivered again.

Ronny had so wanted to be Martin's love and belong to him permanently, and believing he could be faithful to her was playing on her mind. Martin's partner had left him only recently, and Ronny wondered whether she was to become the result of his testing out the market, so to speak. His newfound status as a single person, even with two adorable twin sons. She could easily be his first encounter at attracting the opposite sex again on a completely casual basis.

The words of the song had echoed in her thoughts whilst showering. They could have equally mirrored her love for her dad and the feelings she was getting about Martin Davies, the twins' father. Her dad had let her down badly, in her books.

Was Martin going to do the same? Ironically, as children, she'd not liked him at all. Gina was the one who'd gone out with him and, though the relationship hadn't lasted that long, for a while Gina had remained disappointed and upset.

The bodily vibes coming from Ronny had completely changed since then. The handsome man, the father of the boys she adored, seemed too good to be true and probably was. A kiss from him would melt her heart, she'd known, turning her into a helpless heap on the floor, worshipping the grounds he walked on. The chemistry was already there. Every time they'd met, she blushed for Britain, that of a fanatical schoolgirl crush. What would the evening's date discover about Martin?

Walking to the nursery, a shiver encompassed her body all of a sudden. Looking around, for what, she'd no idea. A moment of confusion, expecting someone to be there, she'd disappointed and scared herself, almost to death. The saying "somebody just walked over my grave" had come to light, and dismissing it as nonsense, Ronny continued to her work location.

Whether her eyes had been closed whilst walking, or she'd just not looked where she'd been going, Ronny didn't know. Bumping into Martin and the boys, Ronny blushed yet again, apologising profusely. What was happening to her? A head-on collision, her body's electricity could have lit up the whole of Shaldon and beyond. Martin laughed, holding on to her to avoid her falling to the ground. She'd so wanted that kiss!

'I'm so sorry, Martin. Are you sure you want to meet up tonight? I'm not safe to be out, you know that.' It was a statement. Ronny had grinned, but she was seriously concerned about herself.

'I will take my chances there. Besides, Mrs Turner is so looking forward to babysitting the boys. She will have the television all to herself when they're in bed. Mr Turner is a sports fanatic and overrules the programmes if anything sport orientated is showing.' A fact, one that his neighbour had become frustrated about for a long time.

'Shall I take the boys from here? You can go straight to work then. That's assuming you are going to work. There I go again, putting my foot in it,' Ronny had said, feeling slightly stupid.

'Yes please, and yes, I am going to work. It's a bit daunting at the moment but I'm sure I will master the job, in time.'

'I'm sure you will, you're super intelligent, unlike me.' Ronny was putting herself down, a usual trait on her part. Never one to blow her own trumpet, ever. 'Come on, you two, let's get going.' Catching hold of their hands, she continued the short stroll remaining to their destination.

It was Mrs Turner who had picked the boys up that afternoon; Ronny had thankfully spared her blushes. On returning to her apartment after her shift, a quick shower followed. A change into clean jeans and a tidy top; she'd also put some foundation on her face to hide the worn-out look that had begun to take over. So much had occurred recently and it was showing, first and foremost on the most visible attribute of her being, her face.

With time for a quick cup of tea and a chocolate digestive, a few minutes' relaxation was called for. Settled on the sofa, she'd nodded off for a while. As the phone rang, causing her to jump, it had been Mark at the other end.

'Hi, Mark. How are you doing?' she asked.

'Okay, thank you. Is there any chance of a meet up for a chat in the near future? You name the time and the place. I'm back to Exeter on Saturday.' Mark was straight to the point, so like his brother.

'I'm on my way out now; tomorrow I'm also out for the evening. Mum is taking me for a meal on Thursday evening. How will Friday do you? We can go for food, or if you prefer, my apartment might be quieter. It will only be tea or coffee, though.' Why had she offered her home as a meeting point?

'Your home sounds ideal. Give me your address, and I will call over when you're back from work on Friday and thank you.' Mark ended the call after she'd offered her address, not completely sure why she'd gone down that route at all.

Ronny had rushed to the café to meet Martin. She was late, would he still be there? Huffing and puffing, he stood in front of her as she'd stopped and caught her breath. His smile was infectious, and she had grinned along with him.

'I'm so sorry, Martin. I sat on the sofa with a cup of tea and fell asleep. If it hadn't been for Mark ringing, I'm sure I would have slept for hours.' Covering her face with her hands, Ronny was so embarrassed.

'No harm done, and you're only five minutes late anyway. I will forgive you this once. Mark, have I got competition?' Martin was asking seriously.

'He's my newly-found stepbrother, one of a twin. An unknown entity as yet, but we're meeting up to acquaint ourselves with one another. I know absolutely nothing about him, apart from him being a chef and looking to move permanently to run a restaurant here.' Martin had known everything Ronny had, now.

As they strolled into Teignmouth, a shortcut from the route Ronny usually took, the fish bar stared them in the face. They were there in minutes. Asking whether she'd wanted to eat in or out, Ronny's answer wasn't what Martin had expected nor something Ronny would have volunteered, as a rule.

'Inside, if this is a date. Outside, if it's just an informal meetup.' Where had that come from?

'In you go then. Pick a table. I will head for the counter to place the order. Fish, chips and mushy peas and tea to drink, I'm guessing?' Ronny's nod had provided the answer.

General chitchat followed; nothing too obscure or inquisitive. There was being nosy and being very nosy, Ronny had preferred the slowly, slowly approach. Martin had studied her intently as she voiced everything, enlightening him with the events of the past few days. A much busier period surfacing and now taking over her life completely, it had felt like.

With the food consumed, a stroll was afforded, along the promenade overlooking the sandy beach and the sea beyond. The peace and tranquillity around her had absorbed Ronny's head and she sighed, letting out much-needed steam. There was a bench approaching and she stopped, parking her bottom on it, staring out to the gorgeous view ahead; the moon, a dark orange colour, appeared on the horizon. It was going to be another lovely day tomorrow; the sky was slowly turning pink.

'Who would want to live anywhere else? I can't imagine living in a big town, full of smog, noise, and shoeboxes for houses. My worst nightmare. All this is free, Martin. You don't have to be rich to be in among this. I am lucky, even if I say so myself.' Ronny was being honest.

Instinctively, Martin put his arm around her, pulling her to him softly. She'd felt comfortable there, not nervous at all, and remained safely in his arms for ages. Ronny had smiled to herself; Martin hadn't seen it though, for which she'd felt grateful. A moment of calm and serenity, absolute heaven.

Her mind had reverted back to her schooldays, and younger versions of them both. The shy, timid Veronica, keeping herself well out of the limelight, against the extroverted Martin who had thought, and knew, that he was God's gift to women. Where was he now, on that score? Only time would tell; too many questions now could be damaging, and Ronny's tactful approach had, at the best of times, let her down pathetically.

Looking at her watch, Ronny had spoken first. 'I think it's time to get back. My face requires some beauty sleep; it's showing obvious signs of disapproval, of late.'

Martin's hilarious laugh had him holding his stomach, he was in stitches. When he'd eventually stopped, the serious face unfolded. He was so handsome, she'd uttered under her breath. Her face was coming out in what she could only call "life after quarantine". Good or bad, the cracks were showing, and she'd not relished the idea of a face full of wrinkles, not just yet. She was merely 30 years of age, no age at all.

'Okay then, you win. I must get back to the boys anyway. You are something special, Veronica Johnson. How hadn't I seen it years ago? Saturday is still on, in the café, if you're free.'

Martin had wanted to see her again; she couldn't contain herself. 'Yes, please. I wondered whether you'd had enough of me already.' Ronny's response was overwhelming.

'You must stop putting yourself down, maybe that's what's putting the wrinkles on your face, and not the occurrences of life.' Before she'd had a chance to react, Martin had kissed her intimately, a slow, long-lasting experience, something completely unexpected and equally exhilarating. The dark blushes emerged for Martin to see, but he hadn't laughed, not this time.

They'd reached the café and it had been time to part company. Waving, they both thanked each other for the evening, and their few hours spent together. Martin's last words were, 'I will see you tomorrow morning at the nursery.'

The working colleagues, next evening, at the curry house in Teignmouth, had noticed a change in Ronny. The introverted employee of the children's nursery suddenly had a personality, a character that people had wanted to be associated with. She'd appeared so much happier lately. Her skin outburst had not once been mentioned, and Ronny had known it wasn't imagination on her part. The amount of moisturising cream she had gotten through of late had confirmed the fact, not forgetting the expense.

Her stepbrothers coming into the picture was an interesting topic of conversation. The twins' father, Martin Davies, wasn't mentioned, not at all. Ronny's mouth was zipped on that discussion, a secret until she could fathom out whether they indeed had a future. A bonding relationship, a mere friendship, or a hatred of one another. All would be revealed in time, and they'd had plenty of it, Ronny had hoped, in any case.

Finding out so much about others' lives outside of work was eye-opening. Things she'd had no idea about or had even surmised. Jack, the only male carer there, was in a happy relationship with a young gentleman called Charles, an accountant locally based. She'd no clue but, at the same time, hadn't appeared surprised, either. A man of high standards in all he'd done around the nursery, always so accommodating and friendly, the clues had always hinted at his choice of companion. A perfectionist, a lovely human being and Ronny admired him for being honest about his sexuality, and she'd looked forward to meeting Charles one day.

The younger girls spoke about their nightclub life outside of work, their conquests on the opposite sex, or not as the case may be. Ronny's grins had remembered it all, back in her heyday with Gina. Teenagers will be teenagers; time didn't stand still, ever. Enjoyment was what life was all about. Ronny was about to discover just that, after years of hiding away, on the pretence that her existence was happy living on her own.

The married with children conversation was noted down in her head for further conversation in the future. An interesting combination of highs and lows, good and bad experiences, and children's stories, primarily. The little darlings, whatever age, were their main focal point, the loves of their lives, and their reason for living. Ronny had listened, full of enthusiasm.

People were important entities in the world. Without them, their catastrophes, upsets and makeups, existing wouldn't be an option. Miracles and tragedies, one often followed the other, provided a reason to pull your socks up and carry on. Ronny's inexperience was about to be put to the test, she'd realised, with so much going on around her.

She'd suddenly realised that, for once in her life, Ronny (or Veronica) was required to help, converse, and keep company with others. It had felt good, she'd decided. Having a habit of making a laughing stock out of herself was something that she would have to put up with for the time being. Learning was something that Ronny was okay with. Laughing at herself most of her life wasn't unusual; she could cope with that.

The evening had ended with a promise of a return visit in a fortnight's time. All had agreed with huge smiles imprinted on their happy faces: a concoction of different individuals, all living in the same vicinity, but enjoying very unique lifestyles. A combination of characters, introverted and extroverted, loosening up occasionally whilst working for the same employer and owning the same caring natures around young children.

Walking back to her apartment that night, there were no tears. Happy thoughts filled her mind before her head had hit the pillow; work, Martin, and her family. All important parts of her world, something money couldn't buy. Recalling tomorrow's meet up with Margaret, her mother, nothing sinister had entered her mind, as yet. Illness and her health were paramount in her thoughts initially, but until they'd actually met up, Ronny wasn't guessing about the future conversation at all. The kiss between her and Martin had sent her soundly to sleep that night.

Chapter Nine

Ronny hadn't relished the meeting with her mother after work the next day but knew Margaret of old, and whatever it was that she'd needed to talk about was important. The stern face at the flat the other evening had more than confirmed it. To say Ronny wasn't worried, or thinking outside the box, was an understatement. The cogs in her head were turning far too quickly.

'Miss, Miss,' she'd registered in her ear, just, her mind somewhere else, in another world completely.

Looking down, Ben and Aaron were stood there, their smiling faces bringing her back from the vortex it had seemed.

'Daddy is here, Miss. He wants to talk to you.' Was it that time already?

Walking towards him, carrying their coats and bags as she passed the cloakroom area, he was a sight for sore eyes, in a good way, a very good way. A smile had struggled to crupt, a severe attempt at it. Touching her arm, he'd asked if she was all right.

'I'm sure it's nothing serious with Mum, Martin. Mother and daughter occasions are far and few between, what with the bakery shop's commitments. Once a month, usually, that's about it,' had been Ronny's reply.

Taking out a card from his wallet, he handed it to her. 'That's my mobile number. I want an update as soon as you get home tonight, no argument. I don't care what time it is. I only wish I could be there with you, to be of some support.' The sincerity in Martin's voice was for real, his concern for her was truly meant, and she'd no doubt about it.

Thanking him, she waved to the twins as they all left the nursery. Busying herself with the normal end-of-day tidying up, it had been Jack who had approached her, all new to Ronny.

'Hi, Ronny. You've been a little subdued today, I've noticed. Is there anything I can do to help?' Stopping to give her a moment, he continued. 'I'm a good listener, honest!'

'Thank you, Jack. I don't think there's much you can do to help, really. I'm meeting Mum in the local public house in an hour and a half, and there's no point in me going home first. If you're free for a coffee before I face her that would be appreciated. As long as Charles doesn't mind, that is.' What had she done now?

'He's working late tonight, I'm free.' He'd replied with the typical words from Mr Humphries, the comedy series of years ago, *Are You Being Served.*

As they'd walked from the nursery to the public house, Ronny had somehow felt a little calmer. Reaching for her purse, he'd insisted on paying and headed for the bar at once. Ronny, having looked around the establishment carefully, had noticed the table in the corner was vacant. The same table where Ronny had met Matt so many moons before, it was absolutely ages ago now. Recalling that initial meeting, a smile broke from her sullen grimace, finally.

Jack listened carefully to her recollection of her stepbrother's meeting, unknown to her at the time, and the embarrassing moment that had linked them both together, at the table they were now sat at. It was a hilarious recollection of Ronny's regular put-your-foot-in-it character. Jack was almost in tears, welling up with laughter with watery eyes, his face cracking into hysterics.

'You are something, you know that. Your personality at work doesn't correspond with your personal life, no way. If I wasn't romantically entwined already, I could fall for you myself.' Jack started on a serious note, before giggling. He was helping her, the informal conversation a much-required distraction. He was a good-looking guy, not her type though. He could be a brilliant friend that was a boy, rather than a boyfriend if that had made any sense.

As they drank the large latte coffees, talk about Charles became a topic. Jack revelled in talking about him, the love of his life for two years. They'd moved in together only six months earlier and were still in the honeymoon period. Charles' romantic nature at home had Ronny blushing and recalling her kiss with Martin, prompting Jack to ask if she was otherwise involved with a member of the opposite sex.

Thankfully, Margaret had walked in at that precise moment, as Ronny had racked her brain to provide Jack with an answer. Waving to her mother, indicating where she was, the answer wasn't forthcoming, and for once, she'd welcomed the distraction, right on cue.

'Hi, Mum. This is Jack; we work together at the nursery. He's very kindly treated me to a coffee.'

'Can I get you a drink, Ronny's mum?' he'd asked, a beautiful smile on his face.

'Yes please, and it's Margaret, by the way. Pleased to meet you, Jack.' She'd appeared okay and calm.

As Jack headed to the bar, Margaret looked at her sternly. Ronny informed her that he wasn't staying all night, just for a beverage. She'd acted relieved. The conversation began on a work-related theme: the nursery and the bakery shop. Asking after Peter, Margaret confirmed that he was good; he'd Luke on the phone as she'd left the flat deep in wedding and baby talk.

Jack returned with the large latte for Margaret, quickly finishing his own, just the dregs remaining. Margaret involved him in chitchat, not leaving him out. All innocent conversation, the glorious sunny day was a familiar talking point, among other weather-related issues. The boats were out in force in the bay, what with the summer season approaching. Shaldon was about to become a tourist hot spot, bringing money into the area for much-required year-round maintenance.

Jack stood up, excusing himself. 'I will see you tomorrow, Ronny. Thanks for the company. It was lovely to meet you, Ronny's mum.' He walked out of the public house waving.

'He's nice,' Margaret said after he'd gone.

'He is. He's also spoken for before you get any ideas. Shall we order food now, before we talk? It makes more sense.' Ronny had suggested to her mother.

Scanning the menu, two lasagne and salads were ordered, along with two portions of garlic bread. Margaret had insisted on paying, Ronny hadn't argued. Another coffee each was also ordered from the bar. The evening had started out on a calm note, Matt and Rose had set the date, in just two months' time. The venue was The Devon Arms in Exeter, a meeting point halfway between everyone's homes, well, almost. It had looked good on the map, anyway.

A public house cum hotel that had conducted wedding venues for the smaller clientele. Rose was sorting out invitations as they'd spoken, a reception being prepared in the establishment itself. Rooms could be booked for the day and afterwards for all guests. Rose will be in touch soon, Margaret had told her, with everything she'd needed to know. Peter was trying to get his eldest son, Luke, and his wife and son, to fly from America for the occasion.

Things were going well on that score. Ronny couldn't argue that neither Rose nor Matt had contacted her, she'd not spent an evening in her apartment this week, and the weekend was looking to continue that way as well. A busy little bee Ronny was at the moment, and she'd no complaints. Informing her mother that Mark was calling over to her apartment tomorrow evening after work, for a talk, Margaret had smiled before replying.

'I'm glad; he could do with a friend here. He's a lot going on in his life. The business in Exeter isn't performing; he's got to get established elsewhere before losing too much money. Teignmouth is looking to be a good move; a few of his viewings are having positive vibes.' Margaret's comments were very welcome and appeared uplifting on the home front score.

Ronny was pleased, and excited for the meet up with her newfound stepbrother, on a platonic level of course. She was still nervous about inviting Mark to her apartment and hadn't a notion as to why she'd suggested the venue in the first place. Martin hadn't even known where she'd lived! The meal arrived and had smelled and looked absolutely delicious. The garlic bread, an obvious addition to the lasagne dish, and a favourite among all the family for years. Their mouths were watering. Ronny had also enjoyed the cheese-topped version, as a guilty snack in the café she regularly went to, and after meeting up with Martin and the twins' there recently, a more than definite favourite in her eyes, without a doubt.

They ate their meal whilst it was still hot, common sense really, nothing much spoken between them both. Comments on the meal had Ronny wondering whether her mother could indeed cook the same or similar, in small portions to sell to her customers. Margaret's thought process was in operation immediately. 'A good point. I will seriously think about it. Thanks for the input.'

The moment had arrived. Ronny immediately asked her mother if she was ill. The response had been a very loud no. The relief had caused Ronny to sigh, an elevated breath of fresh air erupting from her lungs. Margaret had apologised, not having realised she'd guessed her health condition was depleting in some way or form.

'No, Ronny, this is all about your father and me. It's a long story, and I will keep it as short as I can.' The empty plates were removed by the bar staff. Two more coffees were ordered. This was going to be a long night. 'Your grandfather's passing wasn't the only reason we parted, Veronica (the formal Christian name had a reason for being implemented), there were other issues. Things weren't that clear cut, I'm afraid.' Margaret stopped to sip the newly brought latte now in front of her.

'I'm listening, Mum,' her daughter had volunteered.

'I hated Exeter, as you know. Shaldon is, and always will be home to me. It's my birthplace, but more than that, it's where I'm comfortable living. That's not to say I'd refuse to follow Peter if there had ever occurred a reason to relocate. He's my husband and where I belong, with him.'

Now Ronny was getting confused. The explanation from Matt and her conception of her parents' separation had now thrown its toys out of the pram, so to speak. Had her mother just said that she'd refused to return to Exeter after Ronny's grandfather's death, but not because of her genuine love for Shaldon? That's how it had sounded to her. The facial expression now apparent on Margaret's daughter's face relayed unfounded, unknown and unforeseen images in her mind.

Nothing was making any sense at all. Ronny stopped to sip her coffee then, awaiting more from her mother.

'Whilst living in Exeter, when you girls were babies, I was introduced to someone, who, as the years passed, I became infatuated with. Always loving your father, then and now, the gentleman in question, pushed my senses over and above the feelings that I'd felt for your dad. I couldn't get him out of my head, the chemistry was euphoric every time we had met up, not alone, I might add. I was never unfaithful to Vernon.' There she'd said it now. Margaret stopped for breath, awaiting a response from her daughter, anything!

'I don't understand, Mum.' Ronny hadn't understood, as simple as that.

'Our return to Shaldon as a family was my idea. A reason to be as far away from this man as I possibly could. If I couldn't see him, then we could all function as a family again. I had gone along with the pretence of being homesick, missing my mother, anything significant I could make up as an excuse, but the reality was my love for this other person. I had no intention of breaking up the marriage; it was a means to an end, really. Living here we were comfortable, I always loved your father's company, there was no question there. All muddled along brilliantly until your grandfather became ill.' Were things becoming clearer for her daughter?

'Keep going, Mum,' Ronny told her.

'When your grandfather passed away, Vernon hadn't wanted to leave his mother alone. With no siblings, it had been up to him to be there for her. He'd asked me to move the family back to Exeter, enabling him to do just that. His old workplace was more than happy to have him back, he was a good worker, and he's still there now, in the builder's merchant's.' A breather for more liquid replenishment, Margaret was getting things off her chest, at long last.

'Go on, I'm all ears.' Ronny's response to her mother.

'I couldn't do it, Veronica. It would have meant seeing the gentleman again. He worked with your dad, and he was a married man. His feelings and mine were reciprocated completely, though nothing on the sexual route ever occurred. We'd both ensured that neither of us was unfaithful to our partners. Our marriage vows were honourable, and as you know, marriage is sacred to me.' It was all coming out now.

There was a deadly silence between the ladies. Space was required and time to take everything in, momentarily. If Ronny had smoked, she'd have taken a break outside the public house; but Ronny had never smoked a cigarette in all her years, so that wasn't an option. A toilet break had answered the purpose, Ronny excused herself, ordering yet another beverage at the bar, this time two large white wines.

Carrying the glasses to the table, she was ready to hear more, indicating to her mother to continue. She'd wanted to know everything, no holds barred.

'I refused to move back to Exeter, on the pretence that I wouldn't be able to cope. Mum was still here, so she'd become another formidable excuse. I'm not pleased with myself, Veronica, by any means. Moving back, sparks would have been reignited and heaven knows what else. I couldn't do it, couldn't take the chance.' Had Margaret made any sense?

'That doesn't answer why Dad stopped sending us birthday cards and money. Why did he stop, Mum?' A question lurking on Ronny's mind, an important one at that.

'He was being cruel to be kind if I'm honest. He loved you both then, and always will. His hatred towards me was prominent in his actions at first. I'd refused to visit him, even to the extent of taking you two to him for the school holidays. I'm not proud of my actions. He was Vernon's friend, Veronica.' There she'd said it. 'I've lived here ever since, wondering if we could have worked things out, but we can't go backwards, it's impossible.'

'Mum, Dad still lives with my grandmother. She's got dementia now; Matt told me when he was here last,' Ronny said to her.

'I know. She's deteriorating quite quickly apparently, I've been informed. I wish there was something I could do to help. It's out of my hands now. I'm all for you and your sister getting in touch with him again. He would love to see you.'

'There's something you're still not telling me, isn't there? I'm waiting!' She was, indeed.

'The gentleman, in question, lost his wife to an incurable illness two years ago. He's still friendly with your father and has forgiven both of us.' Could Ronny add the numbers up?

The penny suddenly dropped. Ronny's face shuddered, and she could have screamed out loud but held her emotions in tightly. Another toilet break was in urgent need, the drinks passing quickly throughout her body, and an added interlude to digest what her mother had actually told her.

A breath of fresh air outside had her noticing Martin in the vicinity. He was walking past, having bought fish and chips; they were still warm in his hands. He walked over to her, no questions, just a touch and a kiss on the cheek. The look of despair on her face was obvious.

'I will wait up for your call,' he'd uttered before moving away and waving.

Ronny returned to the table, where another white wine was waiting for her. She acknowledged the much-needed drink, sipping it instantly. 'Were you and Peter in touch before he walked into the bakery shop last year? The truth, Mum.'

'No, that is the truth. I was prepared to live without a man by my side for the rest of my life. After his wife's death, Peter asked Vernon for my address and revealed his true feelings towards me all along. Your dad was shocked but had understood the reason for my refusal to return to Exeter, knowing the score. They are still friends, Veronica. He admires the fact that neither of us went behind his back, kept our distances, even though it broke our marriage up.' A short reprieve followed. 'Say something, please.'

'I don't know what to say, Mum.' She hadn't. Words were lost.

'Can you pass the message on to Virginia, please? I'm not up to repeating it all again. Peter and I are happy, very happy. Find your match, Veronica, and enjoy life as a couple. My only recommendation is to make sure he lights up all your senses, one chance you've got. Jack seemed nice; he's not the one for you.'

Ronny laughed very loudly before replying. 'He has a partner, as I told you before. His name is Charles, Mum, known affectionately to his friends as Charlie.' Her head had suddenly cleared and she hugged her mother without thinking. 'I'm glad it's all out in the open now. That took some guts and I'm more than proud of you.' Ronny had meant every word.

Chapter Ten

Ronny walked into her apartment, throwing her coat onto the sofa, slumping into the single chair nearest to her, exhausted. The kettle remained off the boil, the amount of liquid drank was more than substantial for the day's quota, and there had been no space left in her stomach for any more. An automatic occurrence usually, her body hadn't required anything else, in liquid or food form, not even the obligatory chocolate biscuit. She'd needed sleep desperately.

A quick shower, her pyjamas on, she sat upright in the bed and picked up her phone. She'd promised to update Martin. He would be waiting for her call. With the number input, it rang for mere seconds before she'd heard Martin's voice.

'At last,' he'd sighed. 'Are you okay, Ronny?'

'Yes, thank you. Are you sitting down?' she asked him.

'I'm in bed, so yes. Come on, spit it out. Going by your expression earlier, things weren't good between you and your mother.' That was the look Ronny had portrayed.

'Mum and I are fine, Martin. I honestly couldn't be more proud of her. She'd held her feelings in for 25 years; I can't believe it. It was quite a revelation, though.' Ronny told her parents' story, in a slightly shortened version, but ensuring the most important parts were mentioned.

Nothing was omitted that was relevant to the facts her mother had disclosed. 'Am I allowed to swear?' Martin asked at the top of his voice.

'Not to a lady, I'm afraid,' she'd replied humorously.

'That's okay then. Holy Cow! How did you manage to keep calm? I would have blown my top.' Martin had reacted.

'That's because I am a lady.' Ronny laughed, for the first time since the evening. 'The next step is to talk to Dad. I'm leaving it a while; my head is hurting after all that.'

'Okay, I will say goodnight. I could come to yours tomorrow night if you'd like, Susan is picking the boys up after nursery finishes and taking them to Bristol for the weekend.'

'Mark is coming over after work. I hope there are no skeletons in his closet as well! If he's going to move here permanently, I do need to get to know him a bit better. We are family, after all.' Ronny grinned to herself, thinking outside of the box. All these meetings with the opposite sex were getting quite compulsive. Was she enjoying the attention? Yes, she was. 'I will see you in the morning, Martin. Goodnight.'

A quick hello the next morning, when bringing the boys to the nursery, was all either of them had had time for. Martin waved, reminding her of their meet up on Saturday morning in the café. She'd nodded as a reply and continued with her day with the children. A visit to the chippie for fish and chips on the way back to her apartment, before Mark's arrival. She'd been so relieved that today had ended the working week. The weekend should, hopefully, allow some relaxation amongst it although she wasn't holding out her hopes completely on that score.

The fish supper and mandatory cup of tea were consumed only minutes before Mark's arrival.

Opening the door, allowing him to enter, she offered him tea or coffee, unsure of his preference. Two cups of tea followed, Ronny usually drank two, one after another, in any case. Mark sat on the sofa, so she settled on the comfy chair next to it.

A general conversation followed: her apartment (she had tidied it up a little), his bed and breakfast in Teignmouth at the moment and the viewings he had seen in preparation for the permanent move to Devon's coastal area, Ronny's home. He talked about the restaurant in Exeter, and that, as a result of new construction built in the inner part of the city, a downturn in people visiting it, and the expected profits to his eatery, more's the pity. The small restaurant's reviews had always produced good comments, but the location was no longer as central to the community and had lost a lot of custom to newer establishments nearer by. His reputation was intact. But a loss of profits couldn't continue, not in the longer term.

He'd appeared excited about two of the buildings he had looked at, all in reasonable vicinity, near the promenade and sea views of Teignmouth, a short walking distance. Location was crucial, he'd told Ronny, so important. He would require staff to run the business, locally. His present staff weren't in a position to relocate or hadn't wanted to. There had been a lot to do and organise.

'I'm willing to help where I can, Mark. I can clean up and serve as a waitress until you can get full staff, but cooking is a definite no. Perhaps Mum and your dad can help there, with desserts, maybe! To start with, it could get you established, leaving you more time to deal with everything else.' Ronny was trying to be helpful. 'Mum makes a superlicious red velvet cake, I'm certain that she could bake an extra one for your restaurant.'

'Thank you, Ronny. Can I call you that?' He'd appeared uncertain as to what to call her.

'I'm Ronny to everyone except Mum, though she is trying her best, and Lillian, her friend and working colleague. Veronica makes me feel like a member of royalty, which I'm not, and never likely to be.' She smiled, looking directly at him.

Mark's awkward sitting position relaxed and Ronny had noticed the nervousness. She'd offered another beverage, which he had accepted, and after putting the kettle on to reboil, emerged with the biscuit caddy full to the brim of assorted biscuits. She'd envisaged her father dipping his rich tea into his cup of tea and had grinned. A lovely thought, nothing negative, a reunion was required soon, she'd said under her breath.

'Was there anything specific you wanted to talk about, Mark? I've not heard from Rose or Matt as yet, but Mum said that the wedding is going ahead in a few months' time, in Exeter. I'm in the dark as to any other details.' It was a fact.

'This is a more personal issue I want to discuss. You are sworn to secrecy, for the time being anyway, you understand.' Mark was deadly serious.

'My lips are sealed. What do you want from me?' It was a question; Ronny was all ears now.

'I've only recently discovered that I fathered a child five years ago. My ex and I broke up on a sour note, and we didn't speak again. You don't need to know the reasons concerning the break-up.' Mark sounded apprehensive all of a sudden.

'I don't want to know the ins and outs, either. After Mum's revelation last night, there's only so much my head will cope with before it explodes.' Ronny was being truthful.

'That sounds ominous. I won't ask, but if you want to talk about it another time, I'm there for you, Ronny.' He had sounded like he was being the caring stepbrother.

'I might just take you up on that, at some point. Go on, what were you saying?'

'I have a daughter; she's five years old and living around here somewhere. I'm unsure of anything else. Are you up to a bit of detective work?' Mark was absolutely serious.

Ronny was gobsmacked. Her, a detective? A loud cackle erupted from her mouth. 'Sorry, Mark. I'm just imagining myself dressed in a scruffy grey mackintosh and a scrunched up, moth-eaten hat. Wasn't his name Columbo?'

Mark joined in, laughing then. 'Point taken. Perhaps I ought to rephrase that. My daughter's mother's name was Polly, Polly Burns. Have you heard of her?' Mark asked, a lot less nervous than before. Ronny relaxed, too. Smiles and laughter well outweighed a dull and sombre mood. She suddenly felt good around him, similar to his twin, Matt.

Ronny had thought long and hard, before nodding negatively; asking more about her as a person, her age, looks, character, height, anything he could recall. Mark had said that she was 30 years of age or would have been, slim build, long blond hair and very attractive, a patron of Teignmouth high school, as far as he'd known. She'd not spoken a lot about her past, Mark had said, trying to muster more from his mind, but running out of anything helpful.

'You said she would have been 30, am I taking from that that she's no longer here?'

'Yes, she died a year ago, I've only recently discovered. A terminal condition, apparently, but other than that it's all a bit vague. She moved to another part of Exeter after we parted, and Exeter is a big area, with lots of people living in it.' Mark was playing with her, Matt's personality evolving from his twin brother, Mark.

'I wasn't born here, Mark. Believe it or not, I was born in Exeter.' *There*, she'd thought, *chew on that*, but she was only playing along, in reality.

'Sorry, I deserved that! My fault for presuming. Seriously, Polly was born in Shaldon, moving to Exeter to secure a job in journalism. She was good at it, remarkably so. I adored her at the beginning of the relationship. Unfortunately, her beauty was only skin deep, and things didn't work out in the end. We parted on a thunderstorm, harsh words turning to hatred, and eventually, I moved out of the home we shared. Later, I discovered she had moved out but had no idea where to.' Mark had said it how it was, no beating about the bush.

Ronny racked her brain, but nothing of significance had sprung to mind. Asking whether she had indeed had other siblings, a mother and a father, and had mentioned her parents' occupation. Anything to probe the cogs in his brain, bringing information to the surface. Polly had mentioned that her dad had worked on the railways; her mum was a nurse, in a care home. He'd not recalled any siblings; either that or she'd purposefully avoided mentioning them to him.

'Leave it with me, Mark. Her daughter, does she have a name? That could help.'

'Sorry, I'm in the dark there, too. An old, regular customer had called into my restaurant recently, asking to speak to me personally. It was him who had informed me of Polly's death and asked whether I'd known who her five-year-old daughter's father was? After he had left, it had suddenly dawned on me that I was with her until just before then, just over five years. Not wanting to dampen her character, her sexual preference changed after our separation.' That had basically summed things up.

'Wow. That's a story. Not quite so enthralling as my mother's revelation last night, but equally as fascinating. Why did the gentleman in question want to know about the girl's father?'

It had turned out that Polly's other half had also passed away, soon afterwards. The deaths weren't related in any way or form, but there was an inheritance bequeathed to the girl, a decent sum, he had wanted to pass on to her. The gentleman in question was an active solicitor and had given Mark his telephone number if anything had come from inquiring about the issue at hand. Ronny had promised to look into it. Mark had pointed out that if the girl had been located, then he wasn't interested in the money for himself but would like to connect with his daughter if proved conclusively to be his child. He, like Ronny's mother, had carried the world on his shoulders, and she desperately wanted to help.

He'd refused another liquid beverage but had written his telephone number down for her.

Anything discovered, anything of significance, was to be shared immediately. Mark had, as well as a restaurant frantically losing money, a search for a new start in Teignmouth, also discovered that there had been an almost possible probability that he was a father to a five-year-old girl he had never met. It was to be a secret between the two of them. Ronny's lips were sealed, well and truly zipped.

The sleepless night hadn't surprised her, not at all. Polly Burns, at 30 years old, would have had the same teachers as her, both being the same age. That wasn't to say the same tutor group or the same classes. Mark's description of an attractive blond with long locks and a slender figure, would have appealed to Martin, for sure. She couldn't ask him directly; she was sworn to secrecy. Where there's a will there's a way, as the saying goes.

Nothing had sprung to mind, what with Ronny being the wallflower, the nobody of the bunch. She'd not mixed with many pupils there, merely got on with her schoolwork, as instructed. Drama, PE, two subjects she'd despised, not one to draw attention to herself. A middle-of-the-road pupil, quiet and reserved, Ronny had hardly been noticed in school.

The school plays, although compulsory, were a huge headache for Ronny. She could act, if she'd wanted to, but would rather not. Musical instruments were optional and she'd opted out completely. Any subject involving venturing out from the back row of the class, she'd avoided, if possible. Ronny hadn't hated school, but her confidence was never good, and she'd always doubted her ability to perform in any subject.

The lady Mark had mentioned hadn't sounded introverted at all, entirely the opposite, but for the life of her, no person singularly sprung out. The Christian and surname hadn't rung any bells either, Polly not being a popular name of the day. Veronica wasn't either, what had her parents been thinking at the time? Tracey, Fiona, Angela, Amanda, Sally, all doubling up in classes. Polly wouldn't have appeared in that category, not at all.

Ronny had hit a blank and decided to try to sleep. She was meeting Martin in the café in the morning, without the boys. They would be with their mother for the weekend. Her chances of having a free afternoon were out the window, she'd realised, unless Martin was predisposed after the café meeting. It would be nice to spend the day with him, just the two of them, she'd thought. A little voice inside reminded her not to count her chickens, not yet anyway.

Too much thinking had caused no sleeping, yet again. Time for tea, biscuits and music.

She'd decided to sit on the balcony, to hopefully clear the cobwebs from her brain. The sea was so calm, the moon and the stars staring directly at her. It was cold, but with her fluffy dressing gown on, she wasn't feeling the chill at all. The air helped; she'd not sat on the balcony for a long time.

A squirrel ran across the road below her, heading for the rocks, with no traffic about, she was safe from harm. Had she had babies to feed nearby, or was she a mere baby herself? Nature was a fascinating thing. As a child, Ronny had revelled in seeing a dolphin in the sea, maybe a school of them; they had ventured frequently in the area, though she'd not even contemplated seeking them out for years. She'd adored dogs but wouldn't entertain having one whilst living alone. As children, Ronny and Gina had had a few mongrels in the past.

One star had stood out amongst the rest and Ronny gazed at it, seriously thinking aloud. 'If there is someone I know there, please help me unfold this mystery.' Who she was talking to, she was clueless, but it had felt good, talking to the stars. The night sky was brilliant, awe-inspiring, the sea quietly swaying beneath it. One day she would paint it, she promised herself, one day!

Another creature had crossed the road below her; she wasn't sure what it was, it hadn't resembled the squirrel earlier. Foxes weren't familiar in the area, more a built-up community usually. It couldn't be discounted, not altogether, but Ronny wasn't guessing. Her eyes were shutting intermittently, and she was now feeling the cold. It was time to hit the deck and try to sleep once more. Second time lucky, hopefully. It would be time to get up again soon.

It had worked, sleeping soundly for the remainder of the night and well into the morning. A hot bath, relaxing after the harrowing day of yesterday, was well afforded and enjoyed. Elvis was playing on the radio again; she sang all the words whilst in the bath. You're so young and beautiful, everything I love, Your angel smile, your gentle touch, are all I'm dreaming of. Ronny sang the words to the emotional hit. Who was Polly Burns?

Ronny somehow knew that Martin would have bumped into her, one way or another. It would have been out of context for him to admire such a pretty little thing then, and not make his presence known. The Casanova of Teignmouth high school would not have missed out on at least trying to make his mark on her. She'd still not established whether the Martin Davies of old had changed over the years, not yet. Time would tell.

She had to find out from him, disguising her questioning well, about her stepbrother's ex and the five-year-old girl Mark was looking for. It was going to be hard, but Ronny would find a way, she was confident about that, at least. Martin was warming to her, excessively so, and knowing from his past experience, Ronny could get burnt. She was prepared to take that chance; the chemistry was there for all to see.

Maybe she should listen to ABBA later and the single *Take a Chance on Me*!

Chapter Eleven

Martin had already settled himself on the table overlooking the marina when Ronny had walked into the café the next morning. Asking whether he'd slept the night before, he'd nodded negatively. He'd worried about her, and without the boys there, had more time to be concerned and to think.

Getting up early and no little beings there to distract him, he'd gone for a long morning walk. Getting up from the chair and heading to the counter he'd said, 'I'm ordering a full English breakfast for myself, shall I make that two? Tea or coffee?'

'Yes, please, and tea please, a large pot full.' Ronny smiled; she'd not eaten breakfast but had drunk two cups of strong tea that morning. The bath had served its purpose, as well as washing the sweat from her body. Her head had felt clearer and she was much calmer than she'd been the evening before. The worry lines were still prominent on her face, a major concern for her. She'd not liked her look lately.

The waitress had brought the pot of tea over, along with a large black coffee for Martin. It had looked disgusting, absolutely revolting, and Ronny had screwed her nose up at it. Martin's glum face lit up at her grimace and, out of nowhere, he kissed her on the cheek.

'What was that for?' she asked, surprised.

'I remember you in school, the little girl in the corner of the playground with her nose embedded in a paperback novel. Your expressions were mesmerising, and I can clearly recall that screwed up nose expression vividly,' Martin had responded.

'You really noticed me back then? You're kidding me, Martin. Your eyes were always on the pretty girls, the blond bimbos as I call them now.' Ronny had realised that her chance of finding out whether he knew Polly was paramount, and she had to seize the moment, now or never.

'I really had commanded that lady killer personification to the pupils, hadn't I? I truly wasn't that bad!' He had tried to defend himself but had failed miserably, in Ronny's eyes at least.

A chuckle was let out before Ronny had said, 'Tell that to Gina. You broke her heart.'

'Your sister and I were two of a kind, always trying to impress others. When she met Alastair, the pretence stopped, she'd met her perfect partner. It was all surface characteristics, and all good fun, in reality.' His answer, thinking about things logically, was true. A nature calling, in human beings perhaps.

'Talking about blond bimbos, do you recall a girl in my year, Polly, Penelope, something like that? She was tall, slim, blond and beautiful, and had all the boys ogling her,' Ronny hadn't remembered her at all and was clutching at straws. She'd hoped Martin hadn't noticed her obvious lie.

'Yes, I do, as it happens. She was a bit of an odd one, but as you said, a beautiful specimen of a human being. Who couldn't notice her? Her father worked on the local railway, he died whilst she was still at school. He collapsed at work one day and was gone! I never went out with her, though I did try, I must admit.' Martin stopped to drink some of the repulsive coffee before continuing. 'Her father was from Brazil, not a native from here. The name is on the tip of my tongue. Pollianna, yes, that's it. Pollianna Santos was her name; don't know what became of her. Why do you ask?' Now he was getting curious.

'I was just reminiscing. Does her mother still live around here, then?' Ronny was getting there.

'Yes, she lives at number 6, a few doors from me. She remarried years later, Ronald Burns, the postman. He's retired now, though. Come to think of it, they are looking after their granddaughter, Abbie, on a permanent basis. She's a gorgeous little girl, huge blue eyes and blond curly locks. Whether she's Pollianna's daughter or from Ronald's children I don't know.' Martin stopped and smiled at Ronny. 'Here's food coming. I'm famished.'

Ronny hadn't needed to know anything else. Mark would get a call later, but not until she'd delved a little deeper. Polly Burns was indeed Pollianna Santos, that much she was certain of.

Eureka! she'd wanted to shout out, but her lips were sealed, firmly zipped for the time being.

The food was devoured with gusto, both enjoying each and every morsel. Ronny dipped her toast into her egg, licking her lips after each mouthful. She'd never been a lady and wasn't going to start now. Martin had grinned, watching her actions as she'd eaten.

'What? I'm enjoying this. I hadn't realised how hungry I was.' Sipping her tea before emptying the teapot of the last dregs into the cup, she glanced at Martin again. 'What?' she responded.

'Nothing. Just enjoying the view.' He'd laughed loudly. There were customers in the café and they all looked around, wondering what the joke was about.

Ronny blushed, trying to hide it, but her actions had caused Martin to laugh even louder. 'Stop it, Martin. You're embarrassing me.' He was but in a nice way. Ronny was Ronny. 'Take me as I am,' she'd uttered under her breath.

Martin had plans for the afternoon, she'd discovered. All boring and uneventful, one of his tasks involving taking the dog to his regular obedience class. Something Martin had taken charge of, apparently. He'd asked her if she'd wanted to do something on Sunday before the boys had returned back from their mother's. The world is your oyster, he'd said to her, with a huge grin on his face. Awaiting her reply, he was taken aback.

'Okay, I would like to take a walk into Teignmouth and the whole length of the train track. The Sunday steam train runs at eleven o'clock I think, I notice the steam heading for the clouds from my balcony, every week on the dot. I will prepare a picnic, and we can eat it on the beach.' There, that was her wish.

'Wow. It's a good job I'm not a millionaire. Money would be wasted on you.' Martin's reaction was faultless. 'Well, what the lady wants, the lady gets. Come on, I will pay the bill and see you in the morning. Shall we meet here again?' He was asking.

'Absolutely, and thank you, kind sir.' Ronny bowed to him humorously. All in jest, as it was indeed taken. She'd received another kiss on the cheek, and the blush had re-emerged. Martin's infectious laugh begun again and they both ran from the café, likened to two naughty schoolchildren.

The picnic had required food to demolish and Ronny's food cupboard wasn't exactly full, it never was if she was honest. Walking to her mother's bakery shop for tasty options for the hamper, she'd stopped at number 6. Dare she knock on the door and speak to Mrs Burns, she'd pondered. Elvis Presley had rung in her ear, with the words, *It's Now or Never*. He was pushing her towards the door before she'd realised, she was ringing the bell.

Thankfully, it was Mrs Burns who had answered the door. Ronny had stood there in silence, wondering how to approach things, without causing a scene. She was nervous.

'Hello, Veronica. What can I do for you?' she asked politely, slightly surprised.

'I'm sorry to disturb you, but can I have a quick word if you're not busy, that is,' Ronny quietly said, petrified and shaking inside.

'Please, come in. Ronny and Abbie have gone to the park, she loves it there.' Mrs Burns opened the door wide enough to allow her to enter, pointing her in the direction of the front living room. Many of the houses in the row had incorporated two living rooms, some had been knocked into one through lounge, but others had remained separate and cosy. Ronny had preferred the latter.

She sat on the nearest chair available, leaving Mrs Burns to accommodate the cottage settee further on. Declining a cup of tea, Ronny had nervously asked the relevant questions she'd required answers to. Initially, she'd commented on Abbie's beauty, conveniently mentioning that she was a nursery nurse in the local children's privately run nursery.

Mrs Burns had probably known that all along, but it was a topic of conversation leading to her investigation.

Cutting to the chase, Ronny asked if Abbie's father's name was known to her. She was asking for a friend, she'd added. With the pleasantries already said, condolences regarding the loss of her daughter, Ronny informed her that a solicitor had contacted her friend and that the information was important. A sum of money was involved, if the facts were conclusive with the answers she'd expected.

Mrs Burns had looked shocked, but concerned, too. 'I only know his first name, Veronica. The father's name isn't written on the birth certificate, but when Pollianna told me that she was pregnant, she did mention his name. They'd separated before she'd discovered her pregnancy and she was in another relationship by then. They'd both decided to move on, her and her new partner I am referring to, despite my insistence that she let the father know.' Mrs Burns had stopped for breath. 'I love having Abbie here, Veronica. She's brought a breath of fresh air to our lives, in the light of losing Pollianna.'

'I know. Working with children, I adore the little darlings I look after. I don't think he's looking to take her away from you; he's as gobsmacked at the news as you are. I can't promise that, though. That's something you would both require talking about. The financial monies Pollianna's partner has left Abbie, I've no clue as to what figure we are talking about, could help enormously in bringing her up. Pollianna's partner, I don't know her name, has passed away too, a while back.'

Mrs Burns suddenly coloured bright red. Lesbian affairs were obviously not spoken about in the little village of

Shaldon. The secret was safe with her. The urge to hold her tightly had caused Ronny to get up from the chair and do just that. She had lost a daughter, at such a tender age that in itself was heart-wrenching. Abbie was the one thing that reminded her of her only child.

'Let me give you a Christian name. Is his name Mark?' Ronny had hated doing it.

'Yes, it is; he's entitled to see Abbie as much as I am. Somehow, I knew this day would come at some point. I've put it to the back of my mind for so long.' Her colour was draining from her face, and Ronny held her again.

Ronny thanked her for everything, promising to visit her soon with any forthcoming news.

Pollianna's relationship wouldn't be uttered around the village, she'd promised her. Asking if there was a photograph handy that Mark could have, Mrs Burns couldn't have been more helpful. A small photo of Abbie was handed to her from the dresser in the living room.

'I'm off to see Mum, now. Some of her delicious goodies for a picnic tomorrow. The weather is supposed to be sunny and warm, from the weather forecast on the television.' She then added, for no real reason, 'Mrs Burns, it's Ronny, not Veronica. Everyone calls me Ronny, now.'

'Just like my Ronny,' she said waving her goodbye. The tears were threatening to fall from her eyes. Ronny walked away, heading towards the bakery shop.

The shop was quite busy; Margaret and Lillian were both snowed under, serving the customers. Saturday, a time for forgetting the diet and indulging in tasty treats and superlicious sweets, and why not! The weekend had deserved spoiling oneself, whatever age you were. Ronny hadn't taken any notice, whether a weekday or a weekend. It had become irrelevant, but her mother was a baker, after all said and done.

Peter had noticed her entrance, as she headed behind the counter, a privilege being a family member. He had constantly replenished the counter with fresh delicacies, cakes and goodies, as they were sold. A welcome extra to the busy Saturdays. She walked into the small kitchenette behind the shop, shouting out to raise hands if tea was required. Three hands were raised quickly, one after the other.

With four cups of tea made, the shop had quietened down, just one customer left in the shop being served by Lillian. A sigh of relief was exhaled from the ladies' mouths. The beverage had been a more than welcome distraction until the next customer, at least.

'What brings you here, Ronny? On your day off from work, you're usually relaxing in your apartment. I'm glad you're here though. I've found a new recipe I want to try out, a dark orange chocolate cake. Are there any days after work that you're not free next week, for a tasting session?'

'I've nothing planned, so name the day and I will be there. The recipe sounds delicious; I can't wait to taste it. That would be ideal for a dessert option for Mark's restaurant, Mum.' she offered. Her mother hadn't taken the hint, but maybe in the future, the family business could help another family business.

Ronny picked up two pieces of quiche, pork pies, butterfly cakes and her favourite cheese scones. Handing her mother a £20 note, she pushed it away, telling her to keep it. She hadn't argued but thanked her. Margaret hadn't asked whether the food was for anything special, and she hadn't offered any information to the contrary. Things would be revealed in time, she'd hoped.

Customers had arrived again; Margaret and Lillian were busy little bees, fingers and thumbs everywhere, packing the goodies purchased for the customers. Peter told her that Mark was going to visit them later before returning to Exeter. He'd more or less decided on one of the establishments that he had viewed recently. Unfortunately, there was no flat above the premises, so somewhere to rent as living accommodation was required. Ronny had noticed that number 12 next door had a board with a "For Rent" newly put up and mentioned it to him.

The excitement on his face had shocked her, Peter never really showed too much in the way of facial grimaces and expressive behaviour. He'd obviously wanted his son nearby, and why wouldn't he? Apparently, Luke and his family were trying their hardest to attend Matt and Rose's wedding. Ronny still hadn't heard from the parents to be, but if they had, she couldn't have given them her full and complete attention. It had been such a busy week, she was exhausted.

Peter immediately walked outside, noting the telephone number of the agency letting the property. Reaching for his phone to contact Mark, Ronny said her goodbyes to them all and headed back home. A quick visit to the small mini market for liquid refreshment and savoury crisps, picking up a guilty Cadbury's dairy milk bar for a comfortable night in; she was more than ready for a few hours to herself, or so she'd thought.

The entertainment on the television that evening was deplorable, absolutely nothing of interest on any channel. The hidden bottle of white wine was found, she'd known where it was all along really, the empty glass and chocolate bar sat idly on the coffee table. Pouring wine into the glass, it had suddenly dawned on her that she'd not contacted Mark. Looking at her clock, she'd realised that he probably wouldn't be home yet. He was leaving for Exeter that day; she'd not been aware at what time. He hadn't mentioned it to her.

Tomorrow was time enough; nothing happened on a Saturday, paperwork or office work-wise related, at any roads. The solicitors she'd acquainted herself with over the years, not that there had been many, worked the least amount of hours possible. A part-time job, it had seemed, in relation to other jobs around.

Her head had deserved a well-earned break from what! From everything really, a week had never wanted her presence so much, ever. Was she pleased? Yes, she was. Had she enjoyed being wanted? Yes, she had. Would she do it all again? Yes, without question. Was she looking forward to time on her own? Honestly, the answer was a decisive no.

She had decided on music, wine and chocolate for the duration of the evening, spoiling herself for spoiling Ronny's sake. The television was turned off, and she parked herself on the balcony, armed with her warm coat for comfort. The sentimental sounds echoing out into the still-warm air outside.

A few hours relaxing, gazing at the stunning views. A couple had walked down the coastal road, arm in arm. Probably whispering sweet nothings in each other's ears, a kiss on the cheek between intervals of strolling the quiet village, Ronny was jealous. That was what she'd wanted all of a sudden, and she'd known exactly who with.

Her mother had mentioned, the other evening, the evening of her revelations of the past that she was to not accept second best. Well, not exactly in those words, but that was what she had meant. Ronny's dilemma had her thinking about Martin's past, and whether she could trust him to be faithful to her in the future. How was she to know? Elvis had echoed on the balcony, again it was *It's Now or Never*, playing on the radio.

Chapter Twelve

Peter and Margaret were sat in the lounge of their flat that evening, shortly after the shop had closed. Saturday was a day off from preparing food in the kitchen, what with it being closed on a Sunday. Meals were simple, cheese on toast, a sandwich, or a simple omelette with salad. As regular as clockwork, their lives had revolved around the shop. Neither of them had complained; they were both of an age where normality had felt safe.

The doorbell had rang, an awful chime. They'd kept saying they were going to change the tune, but time had never allowed it. Mark, as promised, climbed the stairs to the flat, ahead of his father, Peter. Acknowledging Margaret, she automatically walked into the kitchen to put the kettle on to boil. The men had needed to talk, and she was happy to give them space.

After Peter's call regarding the house for rent next door, he had immediately contacted the agent and a viewing was arranged for Monday, later in the afternoon. It had meant Mark returning to Teignmouth for an overnight stay at the bed and breakfast afterwards, but in the light of a permanent move in the near future, chaos was unavoidable, for the time being.

Discussions about the restaurant Mark had put an offer on, a ten-year leasehold, and affordable once the existing restaurant in Exeter had been given notice on, it had all sounded plausible. The added expense of renting living accommodation had been taken into account. Staffing the establishment would be the next step, but one step at a time. First things first.

'Ronny has offered to help out as a cleaner and engage in waitress services until I can get enough staff in the evenings. The cooking side, she has declined. Can you put a postcard in the window of the shop, for any interested locals looking for work?' Mark asked, thinking things through.

'A good idea, Son. I will sort that out tomorrow. Matt has almost sorted the wedding arrangements out, by the way. It's not long now; the restaurant here could at least be in your hands by then. The house next door, if it suits, could be all sorted, too.' Peter was thinking outside the box. Timing was all-important.

Time for tea and cakes, Mark hadn't refused the coconut fancies offered, along with the mug of tea. 'Mmmm, these are tasty, Margaret. I could do with your help on the dessert front, but you've enough on your plate with the bakery shop.' It was a statement, with room for negotiation.

'Has Ronny been talking to you, Mark? She'd mentioned something similar earlier today.' Margaret had smiled. 'I will help all I can, where I can.'

'Thank you, it would only be until I can get fully established. With your expertise on the baking front, the customers may not want your culinary delights to stop,' he'd added, complimenting her cooking attributes.

Margaret smiled at his comment, then paused awhile before looking directly at Mark. Not sure whether she should include him in the recent discussions between her and Peter, she'd thrown caution to the wind and uttered, 'What the heck,' under her breath.

'Mark, your dad and I have been talking. With Matt and Rose getting married in Exeter, we would like to invite Vernon, my ex-husband, to the wedding. He was your dad's best friend, and we've spoken lately on the phone. There is no animosity between us anymore; life has taken a different route for which he has accepted.' Margaret's words stopped, trying to say what she'd needed to express, simply. 'I want my girls to see their dad again, but I would like it to be a surprise for them.' Mark had understood.

'Don't worry on that score. My lips are sealed. I will keep Ronny preoccupied and steer her away from contacting him if I can.' He'd known exactly how to accomplish that.

Margaret's smile had said it all. Offering him another coconut fancy, she endeavoured to make another brew in the kitchen. Things were going to turn out okay; she could feel it in her bones. As Mark had left to return to Exeter, to check on his restaurant there, the "oldies" had smiled lovingly at one another. Life was good, oh so good.

With the picnic all sorted and packed neatly in her wicker hamper, Ronny walked to the café to meet Martin. Being a tourist area, the café had remained open seven days a week. Students mainly ran the place on a Sunday; food was snack-based and they were more than capable of managing what was on offer. Martin was sat inside, drinking a black coffee. Rufus was with him.

'Hi, you don't mind Rufus tagging along, do you? I can take him back home if you'd prefer.' Martin had left the decision up to her.

'No, that's fine by me. He's owed a day out as much as the rest of us. The steam train runs at eleven o'clock on the dot, so, if you're ready we need to get a move on.' Ronny was taking charge, very unlike her. The men in her life were bringing out the worst in her character, or the best, whichever had suited.

Martin had stood up and saluted her, adding with a cackle in his voice. 'Yes, Mam.'

The youngsters behind the counter had glanced over grinning amongst themselves. As they walked out of the café, Ronny had said to him sternly, before the laughter lines began to rock to and fro, 'We're going to get barred if we carry on like this. Where are we going to meet up then?' Ronny had suddenly realised what she'd said. Inevitably, at some point, Martin would have to visit her apartment. She couldn't ban him from her home forever, could she?

The walk hadn't taken that long, not really. A few five-minute stops for Rufus to rest, his tongue visible from his mouth as he panted away. The sun wasn't out, but it had started to peep through the clouds, so a good day was definitely in the air. Ronny had packed bottles of water; Rufus could share theirs, later. His doleful eyes looked up at her, awaiting some attention. Who could refuse to pat his head, not Ronny?

Reaching the end of the train line, from the beach's point, several people were waiting for the experience, too. She wasn't on her own, by any means. Martin could snigger all he'd liked; Ronny wasn't unique in any way, shape or form.

People armed with fold-up canvas stools to sit on while they waited, the zoom lens on their cameras were poised ready to shoot the iconic steam train and its occupants, however many there were. Blink and they would have missed it, for sure.

The noise had been heard, it was on its way. Chug, chug, chug. Toot, toot, toot. The engine came into view, its steam emitting way up into the clouds. The driver waved to the onlookers, along with the few passengers Ronny had espied. A creature of habit, she waved back; she wasn't the only one either.

Mad as a hatter, dull as a dormouse, she'd not cared. It was a memorable experience, up close and personal. Martin pulled her to him, cuddling up to her, Rufus had barked for England, and the applause was contagious. Little things please little minds, had come to her head. If she was regarded as little, in whatever context people had wanted to describe her, then so be it. Ronny was more than happy with her lot.

The crowds disappeared far too quickly, the train out of sight even quicker. Martin had refrained from saying a word, knowing that anything detrimental spoken would result in an insult towards him. He had just grinned at her like a Cheshire cat, which, in retrospect had probably been worse. Ronny's idea of entertainment had amused him, but he'd gone along with it, for her sake.

Decisions as to where to sit and eat their picnic had Ronny dithering; the expanse of the beach was huge. The bodies sat or walking along it was minimal. Why it had taken so long to make a choice that was a woman's prerogative. Eventually, she'd found a bench overlooking the beach, mere metres away from the golden sand. Recalling her childhood and sandwiches filled with gritted sand, when eating on the beach, she'd pulled a jib (a facial expression her mother had always noted) and thought otherwise. The bench was perfect, and the sun had poked its head through the clouds even more. Rufus had required a drink, but she'd not brought anything to put the water in for him, not knowing that Rufus was joining them, in her defence.

The shop behind her had sold everything beach orientated: buckets, spades, plastic balls, etc.

Getting up she marched over to its front entrance with her purse in her hand, leaving Martin and the dog looking at her speechless. Where was she going now? Women were a law unto themselves.

Quickly returning with a plastic bowl, and a small ball, she'd emptied the water into it for the very thirsty canine. Martin had nodded his head in dismay, but had kissed her on the cheek, yet again. This was getting to be a habit.

The food was devoured bit by bit. Martin's appetite well outweighed Ronny's, and Rufus's pleading had her secretly passing small morsels to him behind Martin's back. The quiche Lorraine was super delicious; nobody could make it quite like her mother. The ham and tomato sandwiches disappeared before she'd had time to decide whether she had wanted one or not, but the cheese scones had both their mouths drooling for more.

The sun had broken out from behind the clouds completely now, and the heat was descending on them, causing a burning sensation to their uncovered skin. Shade was required unless they'd been happy to turn into lobsters. Ronny's skin was fair and hadn't tanned easily. Her face always caught it, especially her nose, as for Martin and the sun's rays on his body; the effects were completely unknown to her.

The food was packed away, what was left of it. Conversation had begun, but where to go to avoid the strength of the sun's rays for comfort, neither of them had made a decision. Rufus had been puffing and panting, the heat was getting to him as well. All of a sudden, Ronny's eyes lit up and looking at Martin she'd made a suggestion.

'I know where we can go, to the ferry port. There's a small outdoor eatery there, secluded by the outer walls. I've often had a coffee there, they don't insist on you ordering a meal. The views look over Shaldon, it's really quaint there.' Ronny smiled at him.

'Lead the way. You're the boss for today.' Martin had wondered what was coming next. He couldn't guess it, it was impossible.

They walked from the beach to the ferry port with Rufus content at walking along. His tail was wagging furiously, probably the longest walk in a good while. As they approached the stretch before the ferry crossing, the establishment in question wasn't open. There was a "For Sale" sign, and underneath, the words "Under Offer". How long it had been closed, she'd not a clue. It had obviously required reopening, and soon. With the summer season approaching, the venue had always been popular. Anyone not taking up the elite position was definitely losing out, big time.

Still able to sit outside on the rock walls surrounding the entrance to the garden, a stop was in order for Rufus, at least. Opposite, the ice cream kiosk was open, and Martin headed for it, returning with two Mr Whippys, complete with the obligatory flake. They both sat for ages, delighting in the fantastic scenery whilst licking the gorgeous soft ice cream. Mr Whippy was Ronny's favourite of the various ice cream ranges available in and around the Devon coast.

Rufus was happy, in the shade, sat beside Martin. A few passers-by had strolled past, stopping at the ferry. Sunday was their free day, their one day off, so crossings weren't going today. They'd deserved the break, rowing continuously wasn't for the faint-hearted. Just the thought of it had worn Martin out. How thankful he was that it was a Sunday. They would have been crossing over to Shaldon, for sure. The little rowing boat would have had at least two takers and a dog in tow.

'I wonder if this is the eatery that Mark has put an offer on. I hope it is; it is an ideal spot for a lot of holidaymakers. By the way, I've volunteered to help out on some evenings until he gets himself established. Cleaning and waitressing, that sort of thing; he deserves the break. The restaurant in Exeter isn't going well, not his fault. A newly built construction route has affected the trade.' Ronny had offered.

Martin was in the dark as regards Mark, her stepbrother. She filled him in on everything she'd found out about him, leaving out the investigation on Polly Burns. That, at the moment, was between Mark and her, nobody else involved at all. The case had still not come to a conclusion, the clues were there and all was going swimmingly well, but there were still issues requiring answers and a finale to close the case up. The solicitor had required a call.

'So, Mark is moving here to run a restaurant. All these eligible gentlemen returning or emigrating to Shaldon and Teignmouth: you will have the pick of the bunch at this rate!' He was deadly serious.

137

Ronny had laughed so much that she was in stitches. The tears were falling from her eyes. 'Martin, admittedly I've spent all the week with the male sex, and my mother. It's not exactly been a quiet one for me. But, I've enjoyed every moment of it, if I'm honest.' She stopped to pat Rufus, who was fussing over her for some attention and then continued. 'Matt was a barrel of laughs when I met him, he still is, but I soon discovered that he was my stepbrother, after drawing attention to myself in front of him, appallingly so.' Martin was listening to her intently, still concerned.

Continuing the conversation, starting with Jack from the nursery, her mother's revelations about the last 25 years, and Mark's acquaintance just two days ago; the pieces were interacting together in Martin's head, and a smile crossed his face, at last. A cheeky kiss had been pinched, and Rufus had barked.

'My dates with men, now or in the past, haven't exactly melted many hearts. I'm not complaining, though. There are two little men that I'm particularly partial to. Their names are Ben and Aaron, their dad's not repulsive to me either.' Had she got the message across?

'Thank heaven for that. You had me worried then: all these men wanting your attention lately. You can't blame me for being jealous, or wondering.' Martin was being deadly serious.

'Come on, let's go. The boys should be back before you know it. When is our next date, if there's going to be one?' She'd asked the question and had waited.

'I will see you tomorrow at nursery, we can discuss it then. Your choice as to where we go, I'm waiting with bated breath. I can't even guess as to where we're heading next. The mystery is captivating, Ronny. You're unique, there's only one of you in existence, for certain.'

An intimate kiss had the icing put on the cake, no holds barred, Ronny hadn't expected it. It was as superlicious as her mother's superb cooking if she'd had to link it to something she'd been familiar with. Ronny hadn't wanted it to stop.

As they both walked home, stopping at the café, heading in opposite directions, their hands were held tightly together. The feelings were there and more time was ultimately required spent in each other's company. Ronny wasn't prepared to rush things, but her heart was telling a different story altogether. The beats of her heart were accelerated, so much so, she'd struggled to climb the slight hill to her home and her apartment.

The wave from Martin had continued, long after they'd separated at the café. Ronny had reciprocated the gesture, waving until her arms had become so tired, they'd felt so heavy. Walking into her apartment she'd crashed onto the bed, shouting out loud, to whoever wanted to hear her. Her feelings of elation had held no bounds, but not knowing Martin's story on his separation from the twins' mother, she'd needed to be cautious. Not jumping in at the deep end, so to speak.

She would question him on that soon, their next date. The relationship relied on honesty from both of them. Any question of infidelity had no place in her life, at all. An in-depth conversation of his past relationships was inevitable for them to move forward any further. Ronny wasn't prepared to get burnt; she'd sooner remain free and single, and die a spinster. Her hopes and vibes were positive, but it's better to be safe than sorry.

Sleeping well that night, Ronny had smiled when recalling her day, more than pleased with all that had occurred. Martin, the handsome, enigmatic person that she'd now needed to interrogate, was becoming a beautiful obsession. The Casanova of Teignmouth high school was tormenting her mind, all in a good way. She'd not required rocking to sleep, Martin's actions throughout the day were vivid in her brain and she'd slept soundly, maybe too soundly.

Chapter Thirteen

The South Devon coast, bordering the English Channel, is gentler than its high-cliffed northern coast, pounded by the Atlantic Ocean. Flourishing seaside resorts, with sandy beaches and a greater concentration of people. Inland, there is Dartmoor, the highest, wildest place in southern England, where ponies still run free and where sudden, swirling mists can envelop incautious travellers.

Many places in Devon having not lost their own identity, Shaldon being one of them, Exeter, the county capital, was much battered during the Second World War but is still one of Britain's great cities. The area around the cathedral, the most interesting historic part of the city, survived the Second World War bombing. The cathedral's west front has fine fourteenth-century sculpture, and the Guildhall dates from 1330. William of Orange stayed at the Deanery during the Glorious Revolution of 1688.

In a nearby alley is the Ship Inn, a favourite haunt of Sir Francis Drake. Nicholas Hilliard, the painter of miniature portraits, was born in Exeter in 1547. Nearby, Sidmouth, a seaside resort, Regency and Georgian architecture is prominent, bringing tourists to admire it, in all its glory.

Budleigh Salterton was the birthplace of Sir Walter Raleigh, the famous Elizabethan explorer, admiral and writer.

Torquay, overlooking Torbay, retains its early nineteen-century architecture. The novelist Agatha Christie was born there in 1890. Lyme Regis is the town of the thirteenth-century breakwater, or Cobb, the Undercliff and its fossils were all made famous by John Fowles' novel *The French Lieutenant's Woman*, and the film made from it. Fossils 150 million years old are displayed in the local museum. On the beach west of the harbour, the Duke of Monmouth landed in 1685 to launch his ill-fated rebellion against James II.

Axmouth and Seaton were busy medieval havens that declined with the silting up of the river.

Today, Axmouth is an attractive village, and Seaton is a low-key seaside resort, perfect for total relaxation. The Dartmoor tors are remains of mountains that gradually crumbled away leaving behind strange shapes, all given names: Haytor Rocks, and Bowerman's Nose being just two of them.

Paignton was once a small fishing village, but now a popular seaside resort, its small harbour sheltering mainly holiday craft. The Dartmouth and Torbay steam train terminates there. The popular train enlightening travellers with beautiful scenery throughout the entire journey. One of Ronny's favourite places to visit was Dawlish, not far from Shaldon, a short car ride away. Its bright red cliffs flank the small seaside town and its mainly nineteenth-century buildings. Dawlish water flows through The Lawn, a landscape garden set in the heart of the town. That's where she'd wanted to go next, on her date with Martin, to feed the ducks on the water. The little eateries around there, and the cake shops, were to die for; yes, that was their next destination.

The smiles on the adorable twins' faces that morning had Ronny asking if they had enjoyed their time with their mother. Aaron had spoken first, closely followed by Ben.

'It was okay, Miss.' So matter of fact, they'd not reached their fourth birthday yet. 'We prefer it here, with Daddy and Rufus.' Aaron's answer to her question.

'We would miss you and the girls and boys here, if we lived there, Miss,' Ben's response had been. Ronny had looked at Martin quizzically. Was a move to Bristol on the cards for the boys?

She'd hoped not. Ronny adored the little rascals as if they were her own.

As they joined their playmates, Ronny asked the question, 'Susan's not going to take them from here, is she?'

'I've no idea. I must talk to her. This is the first I've heard of it.' Martin changed the subject and asked if she was okay. Ronny had indicated positively, smiling. 'I'm not able to take you out again until Saturday, I'm afraid. There is no obedience class for Rufus: the trainer is on holiday so, the world is yours for the taking. Have you thought about where we are going to go yet?' He had looked at her, waiting for a response.

'Yes, I have actually. Can you take me to Dawlish, please? We can feed the ducks on The Lawn and savour one of the ginormous cakes in the bakery shop there, with a coffee to take out. There are plenty of benches to sit on around the water.' Ronny's wishes for their next date had been explained in full detail.

Martin's loud laughter had all the nursery staff looking around. What had been so funny? They returned to their role of caring for the children and he'd still had a grin as wide as Tower Bridge across his face.

'You never cease to amaze me, you know that. Okay, what Lola wants, Lola gets. I will see you later. Bye for now.' He headed for Teignmouth, and work.

Jack had asked Ronny if she'd enjoyed her weekend, and he was curious about her discussion with the twins' father that morning. Ronny hadn't offered anything he could turn into gossip but had said that her weekend was okay, nothing to write home about. Not exactly the truth!

Margaret was eager to try out her new recipe and rang Ronny, wondering when to organise the taster evening. 'I'm not busy any evening, Mum,' she'd said. 'You arrange it with Lillian and Michael, then let me know when to turn up with the fish and chip suppers, okay?'

'Okay, thanks, Ronny. Speak to you soon.' Margaret rang off, leaving her to return to the children for the remainder of the shift.

The day, having finished had left her bereft at not having any ultimate engagements to attend. Walking home, a call to Mark was required after her evening meal, though she wasn't even sure if she was hungry. Her stepbrother had needed an update on Polly Burns, or Pollianna Santos, her real name. The next step there was up to Mark, and getting in touch with the solicitor.

Passing the chippie, she'd decided on a small portion of chips, enough to sustain her appetite. She still wasn't hungry but knew she'd needed to eat something. Having bread in the apartment, a chip sandwich with brown sauce had sounded like something she could manage. With enough milk in the fridge, numerous cups of tea would fill in the empty spots of her stomach.

Ronny had hardly finished her food when the doorbell had rung. She'd not been expecting anybody, had she? Walking down the stairs to the front door, Mark had stood there.

'I was about to call you, after finishing my cup of tea. Come on up.' Ronny had led the way.

'Thank you. I'm back, Ronny, like a bad penny.' He was joking, as usual.

Offering him a beverage, he'd politely refused, explaining his reason for intruding on her privacy. 'I've viewed the house next door to the bakery shop. I'm taking it. It needs a woman's touch to make it personal, but otherwise, it's ideal for my requirements. A bit on the old-fashioned side, décor wise, but that's my preference as opposed to the new minimalist look.'

Ronny was excited and had shown it. A hug was in order, a brotherly hug at that. 'It is going to be great having a brother around, I'm so looking forward to it. Do you want me to pretty up the little house for you, when you get the keys?'

'Yes, please. I was hoping you would take the hint. I'm no good at that kind of thing. The restaurant bid is looking promising, by the way. They've accepted my offer. Now to hand in my notice on the one in Exeter and the ball will start to roll!' Mark was happy; it had shown all over his face. The elation had extended to Ronny, too.

Ronny had suddenly realised that number 12 wasn't exactly a million miles away from number 6, where his daughter was living. How was this going to pan out? It would be difficult, and she'd needed to explain in detail. The kettle was put on to boil, to replenish her cup and make an extra cup for Mark, not even giving him the option. With the tea made, she placed them on the coffee table and sat down next to Mark.

'There is a problem, Mark. Your daughter will be living only doors away from you,' Ronny had said to him.

'What! You've found out something. Please tell me, Ronny.' The serious Mark had emerged, and knowing there was one had been good to know.

'Okay, listen good. Pollianna Santos, or Polly Burns as you knew her, lived at number 6 with her mother and stepfather before moving to Exeter. Mrs Burns knew she was pregnant, and Pollianna had told her who the father was. His name is Mark. She's been waiting for this day, with trepidation, but was completely honest with me.' Taking the photo of his daughter from the dresser, she handed it to Mark. 'Her name is Abbie and she's adorable.'

Mark was almost in tears. 'I can't believe you've found her. Does she want to see me?' he asked.

'She still doesn't know about you, Mark. Perhaps the solicitor should be contacted first. Mrs Burns is worried that you will take her away from them. They idolise her, she's their world now that Pollianna has gone. There weren't any other children. Her real father worked on the railways and died young. She was in my year at school, but I don't recall her.' Ronny stopped to finish her tea.

'Wow, Ronny. You're absolutely brilliant, I can't thank you enough. How did you find out, if you hadn't remembered Polly?'

'That's my secret for now. Mrs Burns doesn't want it paraded around Shaldon that her daughter had been in a relationship with a lady, it would be catastrophic around here, a true talking point. Am I getting the message across?' She was staring at him, confirming that he had indeed understood.

'Yes, Mam. Heard and understood,' he'd replied, a huge grin adorning his face. 'I will take all the blame; they don't know me from Adam here. I've got broad shoulders.'

Ronny's vindictive laugh had returned, recalling Martin's salute at the café the day before. Mark had had no idea why she was laughing but had joined in regardless. She asked him why Abbie hadn't remained with Pollianna's other half after her death. Had the solicitor divulged that information at all to him?

'Yes, she was classified as disabled, and unable to care for her properly on her own. Her health had deteriorated after Polly's death, but an unfortunate accident had taken her life. That's what I was told. I'm happy for her to remain living with them, Ronny. Unsettling her again would be cruel. Besides, we will be neighbours, so she can see me often.' Mark had said it as it was. 'I will call the solicitor tomorrow morning. We can go from there, and it's still hush-hush for now. The grey mackintosh and moth-eaten hat stay on, okay!' He was laughing at her now and excited too. His Christmas's were all coming at once.

Mark said his goodbyes, heading to Teignmouth and the bed and breakfast for the night.

Ronny wouldn't have a problem sleeping tonight, no issues at all on her mind, or so she'd thought. She'd forgotten to ask if the establishment in Teignmouth he was hopefully signing for was the idyllic restaurant next to the ferry port. That could wait another day; she'd told herself before laying her head on the pillow for the night and sleeping like a log.

The taster at her mother's was to go ahead on Friday; Margaret had rung her that afternoon, during her lunch break. The normal five members as far as she'd known; if more bodies were to be included then her mother would let her know nearer the date. The dark chocolate orange cake was something she was looking forward to baking, profits on its sales could make a difference in the shop if it had passed the test. The total price of the ingredients wasn't too expensive in comparison to other luxury cakes.

Ronny now had a few evenings to herself it had seemed. Mark had returned to Exeter that morning until, whenever. The solicitor's call should have been made by now, but until it had, nothing further could be done on the Abbie case. She felt lost, all of a sudden, out on a limb. There were no plans in the pipeline, no one to meet, nothing to say. Ronny was bored.

Music and a night on the balcony looking at the stars, she'd decided. A chill night in to clear her busy brain. A bottle of white wine was purchased in the shop on the way home, a good one, and an extra companion to her apartment, different from her regular brew and chocolate biscuits. A change was as good as a rest, her excuse, and she was sticking to it.

Food equated to a microwave meal, sausage and onion gravy and mashed potato. A stable, solid diet and one Ronny had eaten regularly. Ice cream for dessert, with chocolate sauce, lashings of it. As she settled herself comfortably on the balcony, the radio was on in the living area blaring out soft tunes to totally relax with. The bottle of wine and an empty glass sat on the patio table and she opened the bottle, about to pour some out. The phone rang, and she'd cussed quietly.

'Good evening, Sis. How are things there in sunny Shaldon?' It was Matt. He'd sounded happy.

'I was about to relax on the balcony with a bottle of wine, gazing at the stars,' she replied. 'So, how's tricks?' The first glass had been poured and sampled.

'It's been hectic here, to be honest. The wedding invitation is in the post as we speak. You've got six weeks to get yourself dolled up for the occasion.' Matt was taking the mickey, all in good humour.

'What a cheek. It's a good job I know you well enough. How's Rose coping with everything? This is all Mum's fault, you know,' Ronny replied. Marriage was expected before children, in her eyes, an old-fashioned tradition, nowadays. Margaret had believed in it though, totally.

'No harm done, Sis. We were going to get married eventually. I've booked you a room in the Devon Arms, my treat by the way. You can beg a lift from Dad and Margaret, or Mark, your call. It looks quite promising that my brother will be living there before the wedding date.'

'Yes, it does. I've offered to put some female touches on the house for him when he gets the keys. How's the pregnancy going, have you asked whether it's a boy or a girl? It helps if you know sometimes, to get everything prepared for the baby's arrival.' All positive comments were spoken.

'We're having a little girl, Ronny. She will be a daddy's girl; I'm going to make sure of it. Going back to the wedding, Rose's brother will be there. He's single and unattached, not bad looking for a guy and might well be your cup of tea, right up your alley.' Matt was setting her up now, how dare he!

'Matthew, I'm quite capable of finding my own boyfriend. I don't require your help there, thank you very much. What's his name, for me to know who we're referring to on the day?' Ronny laughed, but underneath, she was annoyed with him.

'His name is John; he's your age and has a few bobs in the bank to spoil you rotten.' Matt was playing with her now. A fit of giggles echoed down the line.

'So that's Matthew, Mark, Luke and John. You're not thinking of calling the baby Mary by any chance, are you?' Two could play at that game. Her glass was empty, so she had refilled it to the brim.

'Well, Rose's full names are Rosalind Mary Elizabeth, so there's a pretty good possibility that Mary could be included in her full name, somewhere down the line. We will all have to start attending church on a Sunday, won't we?' His roar had Ronny in stitches. She eased off a bit then.

'Sorry, Matt. Mary is a lovely name anyway, preferential to Pollianna.' Why had she said that?

She wasn't thinking straight. Ronny could have swallowed herself up. Another glass of wine was poured, only dregs now remaining.

'Absolutely. Have you been reading children's stories? Of course, you have, you work in a nursery. There must be some peculiar names in the books you read to them.' He'd answered his own question and ultimately saved the day.

Ronny wiped her brow, taking another gulp of wine. The stars were staring at her, one directly encompassing her completely. She was mesmerised, and a little inebriated as well, if she'd been honest to herself. Most of the bottle had gone without her realising it.

'Keep me updated, Matt. I'm going in now before I'm beamed up into space by an alien. Speak to you soon.' She put the phone down, knowing she'd very nearly blown her cover and put her foot right into it regarding the Abbie investigation.

Time for a soak in the bath, and an earlier than normal night. The effects of the wine would tell on her in the morning, for sure. She wasn't used to drinking so much so quickly. Beating herself up for almost revealing Mark's secret, a bottle of wine during the week hadn't been such a good idea, after all, had it?

Chapter Fourteen

Surprisingly, Ronny's head had been fine the following morning as she headed for the nursery, and work. Mrs Turner had brought Ben and Adam to her that morning, she'd not known where Martin was and didn't like to ask. As the day was coming to an end, it was Mrs Turner that had picked them up as well. Ronny was a little concerned but hadn't wanted to appear nosy.

If it had been anything important, Martin would ring her later, she'd hoped. Walking back to her apartment, with the weather hot and the sun shining, she'd not wanted to go directly home. The Ness's outside seating area had opened later now for beverages, so Ronny ordered a large latte and found a vacant bench to sit on. Enjoying the views, all really familiar to her, visions of the past had crossed her mind.

The evenings spent alone, on a more than regular basis was about the existence of her life, thus far (apart from the past few weeks, that was). A continuance on that path would see no change in the future; a calm and stress-free life admittedly, but oh so boring. The recent past had opened up so many avenues, brought out her confidence and her schoolgirl wit. She hadn't always been the model child, ask her mother.

Martin was on her mind when the phone had rung. Expecting it to be him, she was sorely disappointed. Mark was on the other end.

'Hi, Mark. Any news, good or bad,' she'd asked. No excitement in her voice at all.

'Not in a good mood, I see. What's up?' he'd replied. 'The good news is from the solicitor. He's preparing paperwork for Mr and Mrs Burns to sign before releasing the money to put into trust for Abbie. I've no idea how much is involved, and I don't want to know either. Once I get the paperwork, I will be down to see you.' Mark waited for her to speak.

'That's brilliant, Mark. Do you want me to call in and see her, prior to you bringing the paperwork down? Maybe, we can both see Mr and Mrs Burns and Abbie together, then.' It had been a suggestion, a good one. 'You'd be able to make the connection with your daughter.'

'Good idea, Batman. Why the low mood, Sis?' He was concerned.

'Nothing that won't come out in the wash. I know now not to drink alcohol during weekdays. Tea and coffee are my limits until the weekend. I'm drinking a coffee outside The Ness, admiring the views before the darkness descends. No bad news, then?'

'No, none at all. I've handed my notice in, where the restaurant here is concerned. It's not cheap to back out of the contract, but with losing money fast, there's no option. Teignmouth here I come. I can't wait!' Mark had ended the call. Ronny still hadn't asked where the new restaurant in Teignmouth was, she was getting very forgetful all of a sudden.

It was time to return to her apartment, the sun had disappeared and it was getting colder. There was a definite chill in the air. Her mood had lightened a little after Mark's call, but with no word from Martin, not entirely. She'd gone to bed with a headache, but not due to the alcohol intake. She was worried about Martin and the boys.

Thankfully, Martin had escorted them to nursery the next morning. Ronny's face had lit up on seeing him approach her. Once the twins had disappeared amongst their many friends, she'd interrogated him on yesterday. He hadn't been forthcoming with any explanations though, saying that he would fill her in on Saturday. Martin hadn't looked that happy.

'Okay. You're here now. I will see you later.' Martin had walked away then, leaving Ronny bemused, wondering what was going on. Wonder she had to, nothing would be revealed until Saturday, and that was days away.

The next two days hadn't brought any surprises to her doorstep. Leisurely bubblicious baths, low lights and soft music had been the order of her nights after work, apart from a short visit to Mr and Mrs Burns at number 6, during her lunchtime break on Thursday. Knowing that Abbie would be in school, it had seemed an appropriate time to call.

Mrs Burns had answered the door, inviting her into the front living room, as before. Ronny had accepted a cup of tea this time, as Mr Burns introduced himself to her with a handshake. She sat down on the sofa, leaving him to take the comfy chair. He engaged in small talk, the weather, the expected tourists all due in their droves for the summer, and the lack of privacy in the village as a result.

'Oh, I don't mind them, Mr Burns. They represent the sort of people that delight in what our community is all about. I, personally, like people watching; the quiet reprieve after the season has concluded is more appreciated afterwards. Just my opinion, Mr Burns. It doesn't have to be yours.' It was a bit of a mouthful for Ronny.

'You've got a point there, girl. What would we do without the youngsters about, love?' he'd said as his wife walked in carrying a tray full of everything tea orientated. The best china had come out of the dresser; she'd hoped she wouldn't drop the delicate bone china cup and saucer. Ronny had to be very careful.

'As regards Abbie, the solicitor is having the paperwork drawn up for both your signatures. The monies will then be put into a trust fund for her, for you both to manage. Mark has no idea how much is involved, that should be disclosed on the paperwork.' She stopped for a moment, concentrating on holding the cup to her mouth and not dropping any of the contents. 'Mark is moving into the area soon and would like to get to know his daughter. He's more than happy for you to keep her here; he works as a chef so has a busy occupation. How would you feel if I brought him with me when the paperwork arrives?' Ronny had waited for a response. Initially, a pin could be heard dropping on the floor, if there had indeed been a pin to drop.

Mrs Burns had spoken first, agreeing to Ronny's proposition. Mr Burns had then nodded. 'Mark is a lovely human being; I can assure you. He's elated about Abbie. His relationship with Pollianna hadn't ended on a good note. They'd not spoken after the breakup; after he'd moved out of the accommodation they had shared. He did love her, you know!' Ronny's empathy was heartfelt.

It was Mrs Burns that had spoken then, sincerely. 'I know, Ronny. She'd hated breaking up the relationship, her mind was tormented. Her new partner was a workmate, to begin with, but their feelings grew to such an extent that Pollianna couldn't hide it. She'd not told Mark about Claire, too embarrassed I suppose.' Mrs Burns had coloured, her face turning a deep red. The subject of her daughter's sexual preference wasn't something she'd liked talking about. An age thing, Ronny had supposed.

Ronny had the need to confide a bit more. 'Mark is my stepbrother. He is moving into number 12 soon, hence the wanting to see his daughter, and happy for her to continue living with you both. As she gets older, you can all share her, if you get my meaning.' She smiled at them both. 'It's a secret for now. Mum and Peter haven't been informed yet. Peter will want to get to know his granddaughter, too.'

Mrs Burns hugged Ronny without any thought, relieved. Realising that Abbie's dad was, in fact, Peter's son had suddenly changed things. Peter was a pillar of the community and looked up to by everyone who knew him. Knowing that Mark was related was a happy blessing for them both. Huge grins adorned their faces, their delight prominent, there for her to see.

'Well, I've got to get back to work. I will see you both soon, and Abbie hopefully.' She waved as she walked down the road to the nursery, smiling. Her good deed had been done, and she'd felt useful again. What a difference a day makes, went through her mind. Now, who did sing that song?

Mrs Turner had picked the boys up again on Thursday, Ronny having no clue as to Martin's whereabouts. 'It's none of your business, Ronny,' she told herself sternly. It wasn't, not really.

Her sister Gina had called that night. The invitations were now posted and in everyone's possessions. As a rule, Ronny had always waited for her sister to get in touch with her, not knowing what shifts she was doing in the local hospital there. It had made sense, not wanting to wake her up when she was trying to sleep after a long and busy shift caring for others.

Gina was excited, letting her know that Matt had paid for a family room in The Devon Arms for them all. Like Ronny, they could live well enough, but treats had to be saved for. Alastair's job hadn't paid much more than the average wage, and nurses pay, well, the NHS wouldn't make anyone millionaires. The details were spoken about between the two siblings, and Gina had loved dressing the twins up and herself.

Ronny hadn't given the clothes side of things a thought but realised that something had to be purchased. Nothing in her cramped wardrobe would do for the occasion. Could Martin take her clothes shopping for an outfit before the wedding? It had been another light-bulb moment. First, they'd a big discussion on lots of matters, whilst feeding the ducks in Dawlish. Now, there was a thought!

The siblings call continued for a good while. Ronny had put her in the picture regarding their mother's new dessert awaiting a taster session tomorrow evening. Not knowing how to tell her on the phone about Margaret's betrayal whilst with their father, she'd decided that another occasion was more suitable, and face to face, as opposed to down a telephone line. Ronny had accepted the situation, and Gina would be more than amenable also. It was all in the past now, anyway.

The bubblicious bath was awaiting her, and Elvis Presley sang in the background. He was a handsome man throughout his short life, and his voice could never, in her eyes, ever be beaten. Those come-to-bed eyes would have been irresistible, in his heyday, and there were so, so many female followers, and some not just looking at him, either! A gentle touch, a kiss, absolute heaven. An impossible dream. *Can't Help Falling in Love with You* was playing as she relaxed underneath the soapy suds, thinking about Martin Davies, of all people.

Ronny headed towards the bakery shop and the flat above, after a somewhat strange Friday at the nursery. A few of the children had fallen in the playground at break time. Ronny had busied herself, putting the magic sponge on the various bruised knees and fingers, and the obligatory plaster usually adorned with a cartoon character to amuse them and forget all about the fall.

The weather had reflected a gorgeous July summer day, still a month or so off, a beautiful advantage. Their enthusiasm at playing outdoors, relieving their pent-up energy to their fullest. Minor accidents were unavoidable, also the odd tear or two. Today had encountered a few of these incidents, but all went home no worse for wear in the end. All had smiles on their faces.

A message just beforehand had indicated that seven would be tasting the dessert Margaret was baking that evening. Seven chip suppers please, she'd written. The food was picked up and was now being carried to the flat. Maybe Lillian's husband was joining in with the regular occasion, getting more often now, and now treated as a general get together. Margaret's ideas were working, bringing more funds into the business, all good on that front.

She'd walked steadily up the stairs, the carrier bag burning against her legs. Knocking on the main door and placing the suppers on the kitchen worktop, Ronny had been right. Lillian's husband was there, sat next to his youngest son, Michael. His oldest son was also there, Martin. She'd not known what to do or say. Margaret had saved the day, thankfully.

'Hello, Ronny. You did get my message, didn't you? David has decided to join us today, along with Martin, their eldest son.' She headed towards the kitchen and Ronny quickly followed her, acknowledging them both with a wave and a softly spoken, 'Hi.'

The plates were filled with large pieces of battered fish, chips and mushy peas. The teas poured out and placed on the dining table. 'I will eat mine out here, Mum. There's not enough room around the dining table for all of us.' Ronny had felt out of her depth, not knowing where to put herself. The further away from Martin, the better.

'You'll do no such thing. It's all sorted. Lillian and David are eating theirs on their laps, with our lap trays, on the sofa. There's enough room for the rest of us around the table.' Well, that hadn't worked, had it?

As the five settled themselves to eat the fish suppers, Martin had ended up sat next to Ronny, just where she hadn't wanted him. Her nervousness had been obvious to him, but not to the others. Small talk amongst everyone gathered around the table continued throughout the meal, even Michael had joined in, unusual for him. Martin's return to the

159

neighbourhood was a centre point of one conversation, an awkward one at that. He'd not let any cats out of the bag. Ronny had sighed, secretly thanking him.

With the food eaten, empty plates removed from the table, in its place a humongous cake was carried in and put centrally for all to see. 'Wow,' Ronny said. 'You've truly excelled yourself this time, Mum. No wonder you wanted seven of us to taste it.' Her mouth was drooling; she'd not wanted to wait before trying it.

Margaret had watched her carefully. She was heading towards the cake, ready to dip a finger on the edge of the large plate the cake had been sat on. There were crumbs that had settled there.

'Veronica! Manners please.' The small tea plates were still in the kitchen, and the small forks to eat the dessert with. 'Can you get the plates, please, while I cut the cake into slices?'

Martin had wanted to laugh, but one look at Ronny had told him otherwise. He returned his face to a near-normal image, on the verge of sombre, just for her. With large pieces passed around, the tasting began. Silence, all absorbed in praising or condemning the piece of artwork now completely obliterated. Single cream was there as an accompaniment if required. It hadn't needed it. The cake was delicious, all on its own.

'Well, someone, say something,' Margaret had said. 'I'm waiting.'

'Can I have this for my wedding cake, Mum? When I find someone who will marry me, that is. It's super delicious. You've got to include this in the shop and at Mark's restaurant.' Ronny had spoken. 'It's a winner all around.'

'Anyone else? More comments please,' she said looking at the others.

'I think, Ronny has said it for us all, Margaret. It's outstanding in taste and design. Congratulations, you're brilliant at your job.' Martin's remarks had caused huge applause from everyone. He glanced at Ronny, starting to head for the kitchen, clearing the plates from the table.

'I will help you,' he'd offered, and picked up more crockery to place in the dishwasher. The kettle was boiling away, so their whispers weren't heard from the others in the living room.

Ronny asked him what he was doing there. His reply was that he was invited, and had replied positively. 'The boys are with Susan, so why not?' Martin's answer was valid enough, in context. She couldn't argue with him.

The teas were prepared and taken into the living area. Lillian and David were sampling a second piece (though much smaller than the first one), of dark chocolate orange cake. Ronny pulled a jib, joking really. She couldn't eat another thing. Winding her mother up was something Ronny was good at.

'Veronica. You should be the size of a house, you know that. There's more fat on a skinny rabbit than on you.' Her words never failed. Margaret was an unknown entity.

Martin couldn't help it. He roared with laughter, hysterically so. Just looking at him, Ronny had to join in. Her ribs were hurting with the laughter and she sat on one of the dining chairs trying to stop. Just one look at Martin, and the laughter began again. The others ogled the pair of them without even a smile on their face.

Peter had stared at them quizzically but had remained silent, not uttering a word. For want of conversation, he'd spoken about the oncoming wedding and Luke, his wife and grandson were all mentioned. They would all be there at The Devon Arms to celebrate the occasion, something he was truly looking forward to. A joining up of an entire family, all together for once, at least.

He smiled, staring at Martin and Ronny again. He wasn't stupid, by any means. The others hadn't noticed their closeness or their chemistry. They'd merely pushed their behaviour to the background, thinking nothing of it. Peter was more astute than any of the others there, and he had realised that there was more to them both than mere friendship. As far as anyone had known, they'd never met before. Well, not since high school, anyway.

As Ronny headed home, closely followed by Martin, a sigh of relief, a huge one, had her wondering about the future. How long could she keep all her secrets quiet? Her brain was expanding, ready to explode. 'That was close,' she'd uttered out loud.

'It sure was,' a voice had been heard behind her. 'I will see you tomorrow morning. Same time, same place.' It had been Martin's infectious voice.

Chapter Fifteen

Ronny had deliberated as to whether to take a packed lunch to Dawlish but had recalled the famous fish shop, Chips A'Hoy. Lunch there and a sweet delight in the bakery shop that had sold the cakes to die for that would suffice both their stomachs. Bread she had remembered for the ducks, placing a few slices in her handbag. Dressing in her weekend jeans, a pink t-shirt and carrying her denim jacket, she closed the door behind her and headed towards the café and their usual meeting point.

Looking at her watch, she realised that she was five minutes late again. Martin, as before, had arrived early and was partaking in a black coffee, gross! It had looked disgusting. On seeing her enter the café, he got up, looked at her sternly before saying very loudly.

'Veronica. What time do you call this? Time waits for no one and you are late.' His face was a picture until the giggles had set in.

'Very amusing, Martin. You are hoping to get barred, aren't you?' Ronny responded with a huge smile on her face, but then noticed the staff wondering what was happening, showing major concern. 'It's all okay here; Martin is the joker of the pack. Take no notice.'

Martin's car was parked close by, spaces being limited near the café. As they walked to his vehicle, a two-year-old Renault Captur, Ronny was impressed. With the boys in the car on a regular basis, it was clean to pristine, albeit requiring a wash on the exterior. She gave him the thumbs up as she got into the passenger seat.

'I'm glad you approve. Cars are a means of getting around as far as I am concerned, not a collector's toy. This suits me fine. Off to Dawlish, we go. Are you buckled up?' Martin was asking with a huge grin on his face. Children will be children, even when they are grownups.

The journey hadn't taken long, the sun was shining and it was getting hotter by the minute.

Parking hadn't posed any problems, though in a month or so things would be a different story, what with the holidaymakers paying visits to the seaside resort. Martin stopped, looking at Ronny for inspiration as to where they were heading. It was her day, after all.

'This way. The ducks first, I think.' She had wanted to fill her day completely.

Martin followed her to The Lawn, the river running through the centre of the town with its lush green lawns and pretty flower arrangements in the borders around the grassy areas. Benches were there in abundance for bums to put on seats and admire the workmanship in all its glory. The bridge, at the centre of it all, allowed visitors to watch the ducks, swans and many varieties of fish from it. Cameras and phones clicking away, capturing the beautiful natural scenery and wildlife.

The place itself created a haven for peace and tranquillity, with the addition of picturesque natural beauty, and quaint shops and eateries on either side of it all. The amusement arcade, although out of character, represented all that was a seaside town. Any resort would be alien without it. A few hours of losing or winning pennies, sometimes pounds, was a holidaymaker's idyllic recreation, on a week's vacation from the humdrum existence of work and all that it had entailed. First the ducks, she'd decided. Heading towards the water near the bridge's vicinity, Ronny took the bread from her handbag, handing Martin a slice. He didn't take it from her. His face lit up, glancing at her directly.

'You want me to feed them, too? Are you serious?' He was smiling as he'd said it.

'Don't be a party pooper. If the boys were here, you wouldn't bat an eyelid. We adults are allowed to indulge in feeding the cute little things.' She handed the bread to him again, and this time he took it.

As one duck accepted the morsel of bread, another had cottoned on to the couple with the food by the river's edge. From one duck, there suddenly became a dozen fighting for the crumbs being thrown into the water. A few minutes of enjoyment, well worth it, the boys would have loved it there.

'Are the boys going to be with Susan every weekend?' Ronny asked Martin as they sat on a seat overlooking the flower borders on the grassed lawn. 'It would be nice for us to take them out sometime.'

'It's a bit of a sore point at the moment. That's why I failed to turn up at the nursery the other day. I drove to Bristol to sort things out regarding the boys and her visiting rights. Susan was the one walking out on them, not me. Why should she have her cake and eat it?' Ronny's face was turning into a smirk. 'Rhetorically speaking, I mean. You're incorrigible, you know that.'

'Mum cooks cakes to make a living, to be eaten.' She was in stitches. 'Seriously though, did you manage to get to an agreement, something the boys would be happy with? They are the important ones here, after all.' Ronny's comments were paramount to the discussion.

'Of course, they are. Susan was trying her utmost to get the boys to agree to live with her permanently, with me being the one with visiting rights. Neither Ben nor Aaron wanted to leave Shaldon, Daddy, or Miss. In that order exactly.' Martin stopped for breath, kissing her on the cheeks.

'You're serious, aren't you? They really said that?' Ronny couldn't believe it.

'On God's honour, cross my heart. They both adore you, so does their father.' Another kiss was in order.

'Why, thank you, kind Sir.' Ronny had to make a joke of it, but in her heart, she was over the moon, knowing how much she was admired by them all, Martin included. 'Come on, the chip shop is open and I'm starving.'

Ronny hadn't wanted to delve too deep into Martin's past loves after that. Why ruin a perfectly good day out by dragging up the past? Today was important to her and she had wanted to make a good impression. His encounters with the ladies could wait until another time. The fish and chips were eaten quickly; she really was hungry and so thirsty.

'That's fish and chips twice on the trot. What was it your mother said about a skinny rabbit, you may just prove her wrong,' Martin said as she'd held her stomach, now expanding with the large helping of food.

'Funny, ha, ha. I could eat a horse and not put on any weight. Something to do with my metabolism, probably. You watch, in years to come, I will be a big fat mama. You wouldn't be interested in me then.' It had been something to say, nothing negative intended.

'You've got to stop putting yourself down, Ronny. It's what's on the inside, not the outside, that matters. Another cup of tea?' he asked.

'Yes please, and then to waste some money on the two pence tipping point machine.' She took out her purse, looking for loose change.

'I can't wait. All this excitement will ruin my sleep pattern tonight.' Martin walked to the counter quickly before another insult had been uttered from Ronny's mouth.

A good hour was spent on the various slot machines. Martin beamed as he'd won on the OXO machine, one with a simple, rather than complex ruling. Handing Ronny some of his winnings, she automatically changed the £1 into 2p, to continue losing the money on her favourite machine. Had they come out of there with surplus cash, no, but they'd relished in the experience.

Martin caught hold of her hand as they'd headed for the beach, but not before Ronny had nipped into the cake shop, returning with a bag of goodies to eat on the golden sand. Still full from the lunch, just sat on the wall overlooking the sea was fulfilling enough for the time being. Ronny nestled into his shoulder, relaxing completely. It had felt like heaven, not that she'd ever been there to compare it!

Happiness wasn't mansions, fast cars, or designer clothes. Oh, Ronny sat up with a jolt, looking directly at Martin. 'Are we going out again next Saturday? What with the wedding in

167

six weeks' time and counting down, I must purchase a wedding outfit, nothing in my wardrobe will do. I was wondering whether we could go into Torquay. You could help me choose, I'm no good at formal affairs.' She wasn't.

'I guessed that. Chocolate orange cake for a wedding celebration, where is the reception going to be, Ronny? The Women's Institute, perhaps!' He was being cynical.

'Not at all. I was praising Mum for the superlicious cake. She worked hard on it; I wasn't being serious. Mum knew that, she knows me too well. If I ever got married, The Ness would be my choice of venue, my guilty pleasure. Matt took me in there for breakfast once, and I had Sunday lunch there with Matt and Rose the last time they were down. The place is pleasant, not too posh, but alluring. Everything I love in life.' There, she'd said it now.

Martin kissed her passionately, not caring about the passers-by seeing them. 'I'm sorry. That was uncalled for,' he'd said afterwards. 'On the next Saturday front, I can't make it; I've something to attend to and Rufus's obedience class in the morning. Maybe the weekend after, would that suit?'

'Yes, as long as it's before the actual date. So, I'm not going to see you next week?' Her face had taken on a glum and solemn grimace.

'I didn't say that, did I? You've mentioned The Ness, how about I book a table there for Friday evening; would that brighten up that downbeat expression?'

'Absolutely, I can't wait. Come on, it's time to eat our cakes.' Ronny's eyes lit up at Martin's suggestion and the huge fresh cream chocolate éclairs were too good to eat, but gone they were in no time at all. She licked her lips, then her fingers, replicating a child's excitement. Martin had just stared at her actions with a huge grin all over his face. Out of the mouths of children had come to mind.

Martin parked the car near the café back in Shaldon. It had just gone past nine o'clock in the evening. The sky was turning black and it was getting much cooler. Ronny could have stayed there all night, cuddled up to Martin, gazing at the stars. The date had exceeded all expectations, and Ronny hadn't wanted the day to end. He'd kissed her intimately as she'd got out of the car.

Reluctantly, Ronny climbed the slight hill to her apartment, so, so happy.

Sunday morning and Ronny had still not got out of bed. It was late, almost midday, what was she thinking? The apartment hadn't had a clean all week, she was disappointed with herself.

Quickly dressing in her tatty clothes, anything would do around the apartment. A cup of tea and two rounds of toast later, she endeavoured to clean the place thoroughly.

It had never taken that long; in context it was just three rooms. Muddles mainly, Ronny was good at not tidying up after herself. The kitchen resembled a footballer's wife's afterwards, the type of female who never cooked herself but wanted a showroom kitchen to impress others. That was a little overdramatic, but you get the picture!

The living/bedroom area was dusted, the wooden flooring mopped, and all piles of unwanted books, magazines, opened letters either put away in their proper places or disposed of in the wastepaper bin, ready for recycling. The bathroom, not a large space, had received a sort through of empty and half-full bottles of shampoo, shower gel and bubble bath. Ronny's collection of highly fragranced bath foams was her sore point, an obsession really. The souvenir shop sold so many different ones, her buys to lighten her mood would often have an addition to the mirrored bathroom cabinet.

Even then, she was deliberating whether to throw the bottles with just a few dregs in them or mix the contents with another bottle with similar amounts remaining. No, she'd decided. Get rid of them. The bath shone, she could see her face in it almost. What a sight for sore eyes, she was putting herself down again. The night cream had helped improve her skin, expensive as it was. The pot was getting low; a visit to the chemist was required at some point next week. She marked it on her pegboard, so as not to forget.

Enjoying a well-earned rest with a cup of tea and a chocolate biscuit, Ronny suddenly remembered the balcony. The empty bottle of wine, well, she'd thought it was empty, was still there on the table, and probably the glass. She hadn't remembered taking them in, not that she'd been in any fit state to recall much of that night. One thing had come to mind, though. Almost letting the cat out of the bag, as far as Abbie, Mark's daughter was concerned. What had she been thinking that night?

She walked out, with her cup of tea in her hand, and there as large as life was the empty glass and almost empty bottle, not enough remaining to fill half a glass. The balcony had required a brush, glancing around at the floor, that was her next job; first, to finish her beverage. The sun was shining and the balcony, at times, was a definite heat trap. Capturing the rays for a while had been the reckoning, but Ronny had fallen asleep.

The doorbell had echoed in her brain, had she imagined it? No, it rang again. Running down the stairs, she was welcomed by Peter and her mother.

'Hi, is something up?' They weren't regular visitors to her place.

'Does there have to be a reason to call on you, Veronica?' her mother replied sarcastically.

'No, none at all. Come on up.' Ronny led the way.

'We were just out walking, a change for us, and happened to pass your apartment. Is the kettle hot for a cuppa?' Peter asked her, hinting.

'That can easily be remedied, Peter. Have a seat, please. I've cleaned everything here today; I've been a busy bee. I did get up late for a change, it is Sunday after all.' Ronny's excuse and she was sticking to it.

Busying herself with the cups of tea, Ronny poured herself another cup, Margaret had walked out onto the balcony. Returning with the empty glass and almost empty bottle, she put them on the worktop, giving her a glare, one recalled when misbehaving as a child.

'That was from the other night, Mum. I was about to bring them in earlier but fell asleep in the sun. Your ring on the doorbell woke me up. I was drinking a cup of tea out there, after cleaning the apartment.' She'd not had to account for her actions but did.

'Only one glass, I see,' Peter remarked quizzically.

'Why would there be more? I live alone. Billy Nobody, me.' It had been meant as a joke.

'You're definitely not a nobody, Ronny. Where's the tea, I'm parched.' Peter was waiting. Ronny removed the dregs from the wine into the kitchen sink. The bottle bank wasn't

171

that far away, she would walk there later and dispose of the bottle. The dirty glass was put into the washing up bowl, to do later. She then sat down conversing with the "oldies". Discussions were good, nothing in particular. The newcomer at number 12 was discussed, Ronny laughing. Knowing already that Mark would be living there, she'd humoured Peter.

'I hope he's not too rough and ready. We must have a cultured person in the village, not some riffraff. That wouldn't do for Mr and Mrs Burns now, would it?' Ronny was teasing them. 'I know Mark is moving in, Peter. He's spoken to me. I'm going to pretty the place up for him when he gets the keys.'

'Really, that's kind of you. You both get on well, don't you? I'm glad about that. He's had a hard time of it, lately.'

'Matt and Mark are perfect stepbrothers; I hope Luke is equally as nice. It will be good to get acquainted with him and his family. What's your grandson's name, out of interest? The twins have never said.' Ronny hadn't said anything out of context, nothing at all.

'His name is Simon. He's eight years old and the image of his mother. Miriam, his wife, has long black curly hair, not a trait in our family. Simon has a mop of head identical to hers. You will like them all, Ronny.' Peter had said, meaning it.

Ronny had suddenly erupted into fits of laughter and couldn't stop herself. She had tried. 'Veronica! Don't be so rude to Peter. I didn't bring you up to be rude to others.' Margaret's stern face was staring straight at her. She wasn't amused.

'Sorry, Peter. I couldn't help it. I used to read the Bible a lot as a child, and whilst Dad's family Christian names revolve around the letter *V*, yours revolve around people in the Bible. Matthew, Mark, Luke, though I know he is Lucas, Simon and Miriam. There's even a Rose in the Bible, I think. Matthew wanted to link me to Rose's brother at the wedding, his name is John.' She stopped, looking at her mother. 'Do you get it, Mum?' Ronny started laughing again. 'Remind me not to call any children I may have from names in the Bible.'

'That's presuming you have any at all. At your age, you had better get a move on.' Margaret had joined in, a smile adorning her face at last.

Peter had caught hold of Margaret's hand, a loving soft touch. They were made for each other, both so suited. 'It's so nice to see you so happy, Ronny. The taster evening on Friday was a huge success and you and Martin appeared to get along well. Had you met up before?' He asked, eyes directly on her.

'I knew him from school, Peter. He courted Gina once, a long time ago. More tea anyone?' Turning into the kitchen, the kettle was heard boiling. Wow, that was close, too close for comfort.

Nothing further was mentioned about Martin, thankfully. Margaret spoke about clothes for Matt and Rose's wedding, as she glanced through her wardrobe. Knowing there was nothing appropriate for the occasion, her concerns were obvious, and she'd inquired as to what she was going to do about it.

'It's all in hand, Mum. Mart… (Oops, she'd almost slipped up) Mark is going to take me to Torquay one Saturday to buy something. He doesn't mind, he said so.' Ronny was lying through her teeth and she'd hated doing it.

'Mark, really. He's turning over a new leaf. He hates shopping, his girlfriend always said so. Well, she's his ex now. I've no clue what happened to her. Mark doesn't speak about her now; I'm not sure what occurred there. Best of luck on that front, Ronny.' Had Peter smelled a rat? He wasn't saying if he had.

As they left and said their goodbyes, Peter caught hold of her hand, smiling. 'You're a good girl, you know. I'm proud to be your stepfather. Back to the kitchen, Mum's got more baking to do. See you soon.' As he left, he winked at her and Ronny smiled back.

Chapter Sixteen

The days passed without anything dramatic occurring. Ronny was full of excitement as Ben and Aaron arrived at the nursery daily, the smiles on their little faces contagious. Martin merely acknowledged her, winking as he'd left for work. The working colleagues were getting suspicious about the two of them, and it had been too soon to come out of the closet, so to speak, just yet.

Shaldon was a very small community; nothing was kept secret there for very long.

Ronny was certain that Jack was on to her, as he'd invited her for a coffee after work, on Tuesday. 'Everyone is busy with their family lives at the moment. The curry night has been postponed until next week. You are coming, aren't you?' Jack had said to her that morning.

'Of course, I am. I wouldn't miss it. Coffee in the local public house tonight would be lovely too, Jack. Everything is okay with you and Charlie, isn't it?' Ronny hadn't paid much attention to him of late. Too engrossed in her own goings-on, she'd felt guilty.

'Absolutely, we are loving life together. Charlie's parents came for supper the other night. They're getting used to the idea of us together, at long last. I'd better do my bit with the children. Looking forward to later.' He joined the children with a game of musical chairs, something they all enjoyed. A bit of competition between each other had done no harm at all.

Not certain what she could talk about to Jack, had Ronny losing concentration during a book reading that afternoon. The book was a favourite amongst the little ones, ironically called *Pollyanna Grows Up*, a sequel to the first novel *Pollyanna*. With the little girl originally paralysed, the second book had her crippled legs cured, much to the relief of the children sat listening to her reading it.

'Miss,' shouted out Aaron, raising his hand to be noticed.

Ronny stopped reading, looking over to Aaron. Thinking that he may require the bathroom, she'd signalled his okay to get up from the floor.

'You've missed a bit, Miss,' he then said.

Ronny had, a whole page. Her mind was definitely not on the job at hand. 'Sorry, my mistake. I will start that page again.' Whoever said that they could hide things from children was delusional. Did the twins know her feelings towards their daddy?

The public house wasn't busy and the table in the corner, Ronny's favourite, was free. Offering to pay for the beverages, as he'd paid last time, wasn't negotiable. He wouldn't hear of it. It was his suggestion, so his treat, even though Ronny had suggested the venue. She hadn't argued in the end.

Ronny's conversation had revolved around Matt and Rose's wedding in Exeter, Mark's move to Shaldon, and her need to purchase an outfit for the occasion soon. She'd not expected the response from Jack at all, but after thinking about it, should have. The feminine side of gay men was so much better at choosing fashion items, hairstyles and were brilliant at cooking.

'If you want help there, Ronny. I'm your man. Just tell me when you want me.'

Ronny couldn't help but laugh. 'Thank you. I've got someone in mind to help there. But if I get let down, you will be my first port of call, I promise.'

'His name doesn't happen to be Martin, does it?' Jack stared directly at her, awaiting a reply. Her face had hidden nothing as the blush became apparent. 'Your secret is safe with me,' he then added.

'There are no flies on you, are there? It's all very new, Jack. I'm not sure how it's all going to pan out, but I like him, a lot. Please, no one knows yet, you're sworn to secrecy.' Ronny was nervous now.

'Yes, Mam,' he responded jokingly, before grinning and winking.

'You men are impossible. Now I know why I refrained from you all for several years. *Better the Devil you Know* is a classic song by Kylie Minogue, but *You're the Devil in Disguise* is more apt, and sung by none other than Elvis Presley, my favourite singer; more handsome than anyone I will ever meet. It's a shame he's dead.'

Now it was Jack's turn to rock into hysterics, faces turning wanting to be informed of the joke. 'If I wasn't otherwise engaged, you would be my guilty pleasure, for sure. He's a lucky guy.' Jack put a finger to his lips, revealing nothing to anyone. Ronny knew that she could trust him implicitly not to utter a word. She'd made a good friend in Jack, an astute one at that. A regular meet up on a Tuesday was agreed, as long

177

as they had nothing else going on in their personal lives. High-fiving the friendly catch-up occasions, they both walked in separate directions.

Wednesday evening had Mark calling her. The paperwork was all finished, barring Mr and Mrs Burns' signatures. He was staying in Teignmouth from Friday until Monday. All was coming to fruition for him, he'd sounded so excited. The restaurant and it was the one by the ferry port, Ronny had finally remembered to ask him, was requiring a signature and a deposit of sorts.

The house, number 12, was awaiting the same, to enable him to access the keys, and Abbie's trust fund was nearing completion.

'Do you want to meet up Friday night for a drink then we can see all at number 6 on Saturday morning?' Mark had asked her.

'I can't do Friday night I'm afraid, I'm otherwise engaged. Saturday morning, at number 6, is fine. Do you want me to call around and see them tomorrow afternoon, to ensure they will be there and get little Abbie prepared to meet her dad?' It had made complete sense.

'Good one, Sis, thank you. You're up there, where thinking is concerned. What about Dad, though?'

'What about Peter? Do you want me to break the news to him also? It would be a privilege to tell him that he's got a granddaughter. He was here on Sunday, with Mother of course. They are joined at the hip most of the time. He was talking about you and Pollianna, as it happens. My mouth was firmly zipped.' Ronny had offered. She could be trusted, most of the time.

'Would you? I'm a bit of a chicken on that score. You'd be much better than me, and he likes you. That's not saying he dislikes me, mind! My mother, Mary her name was, always cussed Dad for picking on me rather than the other two. It was my fault though; I was the naughtiest.' Mark finished and roared down the phone just thinking about his antics as a child.

'Your mother's name was Mary. Matt never said when I spoke to him last. Isn't the name Abigail in the Bible, too?' Ronny asked him.

'I think so, why? You talk in riddles most of the time. Who's the lucky guy on Friday night then, it must be a man for you to turn me down.' Mark had started again, causing Ronny to join in. She couldn't have a civil conversation with either of the twins, that hadn't ended in laughter. Who could be miserable around them?

'That's for me to know and you not to,' was her answer. 'I will see you Saturday morning. I will text you if all is okay, I'm sure it will be.'

Thursday was about to become manic, she'd realised. Bring it on, she'd told herself as she'd readied herself to get into bed. The bearer of good news was right up her alley. She was looking forward to the day ahead as she snuggled into her duvet, dreaming of Martin, a regular pattern now. The usual wink from Martin that morning had Ronny grinning to herself. Jack had joined her, whispering in her ear. 'Your secret is safe with me.' How could she ever be miserable again?

As the nursery closed up for the afternoon, she headed for number 6, knocking on the door apprehensively. Mrs Burns answered it, with a little girl nestled into her apron stood next to her. 'You must be Abbie, pleased to meet you. My name is Ronny.'

Abbie looked a little confused, as Ronny walked into the house, the front room once more. 'My granddad is Ronny,' she said loudly.

'There can be two Ronnys, you know. My longer name is Veronica; you can call me that if you want to.' Anything to avoid confusion.

'Yes, please. Veronica is a nice name. I've got a new doll; Grandma bought it for me, look. I'm going to call her Veronica.' Abbie handed her the doll to admire, giving it back to her as Mrs Burns told her to go into the garden with her granddad so that she could talk to Ronny privately. Ronny arranged the meet up for Saturday morning; they weren't otherwise engaged, thankfully. Reassuring her that Mark was a decent person who would love Abbie and spoil her rotten, a hug was received from her. Her happiness shone through.

'I'm about to visit Mum and Peter. Mark wants me to fill Peter in on his new granddaughter, so expect lots of visitors in the future.' Ronny focused on Mrs Burns, who suddenly became still and worried.

'Oh, I'd better do a spring clean then, hadn't I? I'm not used to visitors.' She was anxious to do just that, clear the house of any speck of dust in sight. Not to show herself up at all.

'Mrs Burns, if this is dirty then my apartment is a pigsty,' she said, glancing around the small cosy room. 'I will see you all Saturday, say goodbye to Abbie for me, she's adorable.' She was, but Ronny loved all children equally, well almost.

The bakery shop was next. They had almost finished clearing up, so propped up with a salad bowl and cooked chicken legs, were both about to retreat to the flat.

'Can I have food as well?' she'd said to her mother. 'I've not eaten yet.'

'Pick up another chicken leg from the fridge then, if you're staying. Is everything okay, Ronny?' Margaret asked curiously.

'Absolutely. I don't have to have a reason to see you, do I?' Ronny was fibbing, but no, she was there to talk to Peter, not her.

'Touché, I deserved that. Can you carry the trifle up; we can have that for dessert. I know you like Sherry trifle.' Ronny had, especially her mother's. She never spared on the Sherry.

With the meal finished, two cups of strong tea drunk, she glanced over at Peter and started to speak. 'Peter, I've something to tell you, a lovely surprise.'

'I already know, I guessed the other day. You're keen on Lillian's son, aren't you? I'm not stupid, you know.' Ouch, where had that come from?

Keeping her blushes hidden, Ronny avoided his words and keeping her distance said, 'No, Peter, it's not that. You remember Mark's ex-girlfriend, from Exeter?'

'Yes, we were speaking about her on Sunday. What happened to her, she seemed to disappear into thin air? I'm waiting, Veronica.' He was sitting up, alert and full of trepidation.

'Her name was Pollianna Santos, better known as Polly Burns.' Ronny stopped talking, her mother's mouth aghast.

It had been Margaret that had spoken next, sitting down beside her husband. 'Pollianna died over a year ago. Mr and

Mrs Burns are looking after her daughter, Abbie.' The clogs were going ten to the dozen. Margaret turned, looking at Ronny. She'd added up the numbers.

'Abbie is your granddaughter, Peter. She's Mark's daughter, he's only recently found out.' There, all was out in the open, on Mark's score in any case. Ronny wasn't admitting her feelings for Martin just yet.

Margaret had held onto Peter's hand tightly as Ronny put the kettle back on to boil. Another beverage was well and truly required and deserved. There was a lot to digest amongst the "oldies", a lot to sink in. With the teas made and the three of them sat around the fireplace with its ornate electric fire, lit to show the glow, though not fully ignited, Ronny had noticed Peter's tears.

Had he needed to know why Pollianna had left her son? No, he hadn't, nobody in the vicinity had needed to know that. The important issue was Abbie, the sweet little girl at number 6. For once, Margaret was speechless, had absolutely nothing to say on the matter. Still holding Peter's hand, she picked her teacup up and drank the strong tea.

Without too much detail, Ronny informed them of the trust fund set up for Abbie, Mark's visit to Teignmouth from Friday until Monday, and his first meet up with his daughter on Saturday, with Ronny as a chaperone. Hopefully, Peter would be able to bond with her after that. Abbie was to remain with Mr and Mrs Burns, Mark's wishes, but with only living doors away, there would be no limit as to how much they would see one another.

Whether it had all been too much for Peter, he suddenly got up and headed for the front door, putting his coat on as he walked through it. Ronny wanted to run after him, but her mother stopped her.

'Leave him. He will be fine; he's got to get his head around it all. Quite the little detective, aren't we, Veronica? Thank you, I don't appreciate you enough.' Margaret hugged her daughter for what had seemed aeons. They were kindred spirits at heart. The love had always been there. 'I've got a good bottle of wine in the fridge waiting to be opened, join me please.' How could she refuse?

The wine was good, the reminiscing a revelation of good and bad memories as children. She'd nothing to complain about, not really. Margaret had treated Gina and her equally, well what she could afford, at any roads. Gina had learned to drive; Ronny had no interest at all. She'd received a car after passing her test, an old banger but it had served its purpose, and Gina had loved it.

Ronny's gifts were afforded differently and always welcomed with elation.

Nanny Joyce had told her mother off for giving into the girls on occasions. Ronny could hear the words, "You're spoiling them" so clear in her head. A humorous smile had sent a murmur from Ronny's mouth and Margaret had asked her thoughts. She'd loved Nanny Joyce, she was sorely missed. Strict, to the point, but loved all the same, and spoiling the girls herself, without Margaret knowing.

A good night had been had by all, though Peter still hadn't returned from his walk.

Reassuring Ronny that Peter would be okay, she headed for home. Her bed was awaiting her, but the good news had now reached the people they had concerned. The rest was down to them, she'd done her bit. An angel she wasn't, and never would be. But today, Ronny had felt euphoric, emotional and useful, a good combination. A smile crossed her face as she opened her apartment door.

The narrowly missed mention of Martin had put itself into the background, not admitted or denied. Ronny hadn't disclosed anything to the contrary. Timing was crucial, but Shaldon was indeed Shaldon. Tongues were wagging behind closed doors. Ronny realised that things would have to come to a head sooner rather than later. Tomorrow was her date in The Ness, no less.

Somehow, and for why, Ronny wanted to make the effort and doll herself up, as the phrase went. Before going to bed, she'd ironed her black trousers and turquoise top, to make an impression.

Noticing the scribbles on the pegboard, the pharmacist had required a visit at lunchtime for replenishment of the expensive face cream she'd used. A war of words, an intimate evening, and their feelings for each other had to come out in the open before they were made a laughing stock in the village, they'd lived in. A secret cannot be kept forever, or could it? Tomorrow would be a night of admissions, one way or another.

Could she sleep that night? Absolutely not. She'd tossed and turned, the duvet was thrown off, then back on again. Her head recalling things that weren't even important. The one thing that had kept her awake was her father. With everything going on, her detective work for Mark, Matt's wedding preparations, Vernon had been forgotten. She'd had enough information to pursue him, find him and get to know him again and she'd wanted to, so much.

With determination in her mind, that was her next task, to find her father. She'd already had the address; Matt had given it to her ages ago. A letter, she'd decided, next week at the latest, was going to be sent to him. The words would need to be perfectly written, not wanting to push him away. Ronny required a lot of concentration on the project at hand, no mishaps were allowed.

Her father, he was, and at 30 years of age, it was about time they had gotten to know each other again. She wasn't a little girl anymore, not the sweet little girl he remembered (well, that was debatable), but as needs must, Ronny had wanted to get her life in order. There was no time like the present, was there?

She'd listened to soothing music on the radio as her head had determined her immediate course of action for the future, one she'd wanted desperately. Sentimental songs with a soft relaxing sound echoed in her ears. As her eyes closed for the remainder of the night, well, what was left of it, Elvis Presley had sung sweetly to her. The song was *Loving You*, and so, so appropriate. Wet, Wet, Wet's *Love is all Around* had followed before everything had gone quiet.

Chapter Seventeen

They had agreed to meet at The Ness at seven-thirty that evening. It had given Ronny plenty of time to get ready, but she was walking around the apartment at a snail's pace. A quick shower, rather than a bath, for fear of forgetting time. A bath was there to relax in the bubblicious soapy liquid, until the water had become too cold to remain there, in Ronny's eyes that was.

With her hair dried with the hairdryer, a dab of face cream before a light foundation, and Ronny was ready. Martin hadn't seen her wearing make-up, so why start now! On second thoughts, maybe some eye shadow, she hunted for her make-up bag, now where did she put it? It had been months since she wore make-up last.

Eventually, finding it in one of her kitchen cupboards, a smidgen of blue eye shadow adorned her large blue eyes. Mascara, had been put on too, highlighting her long eyelashes and rouge to emphasise her cheekbones. That had only left lipstick: that was put on as well. A pair of silver dangling earrings had completed the look.

Looking in the mirror, she had surprised herself, it had suited her. A further brush through her shoulder-length brown hair and Ronny walked through her front door, heading towards The Ness. Martin was waiting for her and she hadn't arrived late, a plus for her. He looked well pleased as she got to the door of the hotel.

'You look amazing, you scrub up well,' he'd said to her as he kissed her on the cheek.

'Why, thank you, I think. That's the sort of compliment Matt or Mark would make.' Ronny had said. 'You look nice, very respectable and handsome, Martin. I'm so hungry; I've not eaten since lunchtime, not wanting to waste anything here.' She gazed up at him; he just stared back at her. 'You are hungry, aren't you?'

'Famished, but not necessarily for food. You're too delicious, I could eat you.' It was a fact.

'Behave yourself, will you. Come on, let's get our seats. I hope it's by the window.' Ronny was nervous, hence the non-stop talking, a familiar trait of hers. Martin headed the way, to exactly where she'd wanted to go.

The waiter had handed them the menu and asked their preference in drinks. 'A white wine please, a large one.' Ronny had answered very quickly.

'Make that two.' The waiter walked away giving them time to browse through the menu at leisure. 'Are you okay?' Martin asked. 'You seem a bit on edge tonight.'

'I've never eaten here on a date. Matt and Rose cannot be counted, they're family. I'm a little nervous, to be honest.' Ronny was petrified, not wanting to embarrass herself in any way, shape or form.

'Relax, it's only me. Martin Davies, at your service.' He'd tried to calm her down.

'I can't recall the last proper date I went on, and it wasn't in The Ness. Can I have the Surf and Turf, well done, with a

187

peppercorn sauce, please?' Ronny knew what she'd wanted to eat, prior to entering the hotel. She'd read the menu several times over when with Matt and Rose. It had become instilled in her brain and had never left.

The waiter brought the wines and took the order. Garlic bread and button mushrooms as side orders for two Surf and Turfs, both well done as regards the cooking of the steak part of the food choice. The peppercorn sauce: a complementary addition to the meal. Martin was still staring at her; it was a bit unnerving really.

She'd held her tongue before responding, not wanting to comment in her usual manner. 'Please stop staring at me, Martin.' It was an order, delicately put.

'I can't help it. Veronica Johnson has never looked so good. Cheers,' he said, raising his glass.

Ronny raised hers too, clicking the glasses together carefully.

Conversation amounted to Ben, Aaron and Rufus, and work. Martin was getting used to his low-profile job, not missing the high life at all. Born and bred in Shaldon, the eldest child of Mr and Mrs Davies, he was still living in the original family home. His parents, David and Lillian, had sold the house to Martin when deciding to downsize.

Michael, the younger son, still lived with them in a two-up two-down cottage with a small courtyard garden. David's health had declined over the years, and low maintenance property was more in line with their needs. The childhood home wasn't huge, but a family-sized property with space for two adorable little boys and a dog.

The meal had arrived and it had looked and smelled delicious. Ronny's taste buds had her drooling over the food before the whole meal had been completely served. The side orders were placed in the centre of the table for them both to share. Asking whether anything else was required, the waiter politely walked away as Martin nodded negatively.

'Can I start?' Ronny asked, awaiting Martin's approval.

'Tuck in,' he replied, taking a sip from the large glass of wine. He was laughing at her. She'd replicated a child being given her first toy. So excited, her expressions were one of exhilaration, he was hypnotised just looking at her.

'Will you stop staring at me, Martin?' Ronny had repeated before concentrating on the task at hand, the food.

Nothing had remained on their plates or the side plates. Ronny's stomach had expanded; nothing new there, it would soon return to normal later. Rubbing her stomach, her appetite had been more than satisfied. Martin offered her the dessert menu; she refused politely but asked for a small coffee instead. Thanking him for the experience, he'd responded.

'You're very welcome, Ronny. We will have to repeat this again, soon.' He was still staring at her.

The coffee had arrived, and Ronny spooned the sugar into the small cup, pouring single cream afterwards. There was a small Welsh cake sat on the saucer, she handed it to Martin, pleading that she'd no room left to eat it. She was full to bursting.

'So, what's your itinerary for tomorrow?' Ronny asked him.

'Well, Rufus's obedience class starts at nine o'clock sharp. He's almost finished his course, just two more sessions to go. I'm meeting Sarah in the afternoon to sort out a few legal issues, and then home to a few household chores. What about you? Anything happening of any importance?'

'Yes, actually. I'm meeting Mark at ten o'clock. He's back in Teignmouth until Monday. The restaurant and house contracts are all coming to a head. You remember the one near the ferry port, that's where Mark is hoping to establish his business.' She stopped, looking at Martin affectionately. 'Who's Sarah?'

'Sarah is Mrs Turner's daughter, my neighbourhood crush from schooldays from the age of five, probably. We used to walk to primary school together holding hands, skipping along the road with smiles on our little faces. Mum had always thought we would end up married.' He was smiling now.

'So what happened?' Ronny was intrigued. She'd wanted to know more.

'High school happened. The Martin Davies she knew grew up, much too quickly. Women, or rather schoolgirls of a certain age, admired the personification that became me. I was adored by them all but treated them abominably. Sarah turned her back on me.' He'd answered honestly.

'And now? Does she still feel the same way?' She waited, forgetting to breathe.

'Now, she is happily married and is now my solicitor,' he was playing with her and enjoying every moment of it. 'The boys' surname is being changed to Davies. My name is on their birth certificate, but now I want them to be known by their dad's surname. Visiting rights are being sorted out as well. Sarah lives in Somerset now, but as a favour to me, she's helping to put everything in crystal clear fashion for Susan.' He reached over, catching hold of her hand. He smiled at her lovingly. He was teasing her with his eyes.

'Oh,' Ronny replied, gobsmacked. She was stumped for words, so picked up her coffee and took a sip. Small talk continued for a long time before Ronny had broached the question, she had wanted an answer to, eventually plucking up the courage to speak.

'So what happened to break you and Susan up?' she'd asked as casually as possible.

'I met Susan at Bristol University, where we both studied. She was the pick of the bunch, so to speak. A second Pollianna Santos if you like, pretty, petite and impressive. We got on really well to start with and eventually moved into a flat together there. The cracks were showing when she discovered she was pregnant with the twins.' Martin's response was honest. Not covering anything up.

'So, is Susan from around here?' she asked.

'No, she's from a very small village in Cornwall. Shaldon is huge in comparison. Bristol became a town of intrigue for both of us. People in droves, loud music, drinking to oblivion and the occasional drug experience. I'm not proud of myself. Susan loves the culture there, and everything Bristol represents. I prefer it here.' Ronny was getting answers.

'So, what broke you up in the end?' It was a simple question.

'You're not going to believe me, but she started seeing someone else, she was bored living here. The affair did finish and we really tried hard to continue as before. I was working in London during the week and home on weekends, but the spark had gone.' Martin stopped to finish his coffee. 'She's found someone else now, a former student we both knew in Bristol.'

'I'm sorry, Martin. I really am.' Ronny's sentiments had almost brought a tear to her eye.

'I'm not. I've got you now, haven't I?' He held her glare long enough for her to grin, before drinking more coffee.

Ronny had smiled, nodding positively and holding his hand across the table. 'Do you have to go back to yours tonight? I could do with some company.' She was making the first move.

'No, I don't. Rufus is tucked up in his bed; he will be fine on his own.' Martin paid the bill, got up from his chair and said, beaming with delight. 'Head the way. I thought you'd never ask.'

Nestled in each other's arms the next morning, the alarm went off and Ronny turned in the bed to turn it off. It was seven o'clock in the morning. Martin was laid there, a huge smile across his face.

'Good morning, gorgeous. Can I get you a cup of tea in bed?' he'd asked.

'I wouldn't say no. Some toast as well, perhaps!' She was pushing it.

'Well, as it's you. Just this once, though,' he was incorrigible. Ronny picked up a pillow and threw it at him, all in good fun.

The next hour had flown, settled on the bed revelling in each other's company with small talk and humorous remarks. Neither of them wanted to get up. Martin had left the apartment first; Rufus's obedience class was looming. Ronny had gotten up then, soaking in the bath before heading to meet Mark at the café, hers and Martin's usual meeting place.

Mark was nervous; the mug of coffee was spilling all over the table, his hands shaking like a leaf. Ronny caught hold of it, steadying the mug.

'Mr and Mrs Burns are lovely, Mark. I get a hug every time I go there; you've nothing to be concerned about, nothing at all.' Ronny was trying her best to calm him down.

As they headed for number 6, Ronny was holding on to Mark, arms entwined. Knocking on the door, Mrs Burns welcomed them both, Ronny receiving a hug at the door. Mark acknowledged her with a "hello" before they'd walked into the front room. At first, no one spoke, nobody knowing quite how to begin the conversation.

Abbie had saved the day, running into the room, bringing Veronica to her. 'Veronica is saying hi,' she said to Ronny, sitting next to her on the sofa.

'Well, hello there, Veronica. You look nice today.' The dressed doll had not replied, surprisingly.

She then spoke directly to Abbie. 'Abbie, this is Mark. He's your daddy. Are you going to say hello to him?' Her voice became quiet, but to Ronny's surprise, she had turned to Mark.

'Hello, Daddy. Maisie and Elsie haven't got a daddy, but now I've got one.' She'd said so matter of fact. Children will be children.

'You sure have. Can I have a hug?' Mark said to her, hoping. Immediately, without hesitation, Abbie hugged him. The moment was so memorable; the adults were almost in tears.

The paperwork was signed and the amount being transferred to Abbie's trust fund was quite substantial. Mr and Mrs Burns were both surprised when reading the contract. The little girl in their care wouldn't want for anything, what with Mark and Peter all nearby as well. Meeting up with Peter and Margaret was next on the agenda, but first, to get to know her dad. There had been plenty of time. No one was going anywhere.

'Thank you, Ronny. That was quite emotional. How about curry in Teignmouth? My treat!' Mark had said to her as they'd left number 6, with Abbie waving her little arms for England.

'Yes, please. That definitely pulled at the heartstrings. I hope Peter is okay, did you manage to see him yesterday at all? He walked out of the flat when I gave him the news; Mum stopped me from running after him.' She'd needed to pay them a visit, to check on the "oldies". The news had been a bolt out of the blue. It's not often you're told you have a granddaughter that had lived doors away for over a year. It must have shocked him rigid.

'No, I didn't get here until late last night. There were things to be done in the restaurant at the last minute. Another week or so, and I will be down here permanently. You'd refused my invitation, not nice, Ronny. How did your date go, Sis?' He was fishing, big time.

'Nothing to write home about, really,' Ronny had lied, but her face had coloured in the process.

'My lips are sealed, Sis. I will call in later to check on Dad.' He was letting it go, thankfully.

The chicken tikka curry, rice and poppadoms were wolfed down by both of them. Neither had realised how hungry they were. Two large coca colas were drunk very quickly, their thirst needing quenching. To say they had enjoyed their meals would have been an understatement. Talk of Mark's new venture was discussed in detail; Ronny's offer still standing as regards helping out where required.

'Thanks, Sis. I'm going to need all the help I can get, if only for places to go for purchasing food ingredients. I'm going to be on the phone continuously with you, you know that. Your beau won't mind, will he?' He looked at her with a cheeky grin across his face.

'You do want help, don't you? I could easily relinquish my offer of support, mind.' Ronny had laughed, but the conversation had stopped there. No more awkward questions from Mark were sent her way from then on.

Monday was the day Mark was getting the keys to the house at number 12 and signing the contract for the restaurant. A busy day for him, what with returning back to Exeter to tie everything up there before emigrating to Teignmouth and Shaldon permanently. Ronny hadn't expected him to have time to see her then.

'I will call in to see the "oldies" tomorrow afternoon, Mark. If you're there before you leave for Exeter, then I will see you then. Otherwise, take care, Daddy!' she smiled as she'd said it. He'd hugged her before heading for the bed and breakfast, for some much-needed time to himself.

Getting used to being a daddy to an adorable little girl would take some getting used to. He was so looking forward to it, still pinching himself. It was real; he had a daughter to take care of, with a lot of help.

Ronny had decided on a short spell in the amusement arcade before heading back home. The infamous 2p tipping point machine was willing her to visit it. It was quite busy in the establishment, it was a Saturday, normally busier than midweek. Searching for some change in her purse, a well-known voice could be heard in the distance. She lifted her head, realising that it was Martin's voice.

Walking along the pavement with him was a young lady. Pretty, petite and very well-spoken.

Her arms were linked into his, and they were both in deep conversation. Martin hadn't noticed Ronny there. She stopped what she was doing momentarily, trying to listen in to their conversation, but with the noise of the various machines in the background, hadn't heard a word.

Poking her head out of the door, she watched them stop and settle themselves on one of the seats overlooking the beach. She had cuddled into his shoulder; they'd both looked so right together. A little boy had run up to them, from the beach; two older people were dragging far behind him. Ronny hadn't recognised any of them, they were a fair distance away in all due respect. The sun was sending a glare into the air causing vision blindness from where Ronny was standing. Should she venture over and speak to them? She deliberated. After a momentous night at her apartment, she knew that Martin had cared for her. Well, she thought he had. The doubts had entered her mind now. Was he playing his old schoolboy games? His explanation as to his relationship break up with Susan, the twins' mother, had sounded so sincere. She'd believed every word he'd uttered.

Ronny had no intention of getting burnt, so she ordered a latte from the café part of the establishment and sat down at one of the tables, in a complete daze. Elvis's little-known song echoed in her mind, the song *Fool*. She sang the words in her head. Fool, you didn't have to hurt her; fool, you didn't have to lose her. Fool, you only had to love her, but now the love is gone.

She was in a world of her own, close to tears, when Martin's voice woke her up, literally. Ronny jumped for her life. He stopped behind her, touching her shoulder intimately. She tried to retract the closeness, but couldn't. She loved Martin, with all her heart.

'Are you okay, Ronny? This is Sarah, my adopted sister and my solicitor, combined,' he said to her. Looking at Sarah, he said, 'This is Ronny, my girlfriend.'

'Veronica Johnson. Is that really you?' Sarah had spoken, glancing at her.

'Yes, it is.' She suddenly recalled the girl standing in front of her; she was in her tutor group at high school. The little boy ran up to her, shouting for his mother. Ronny smiled at him, still in a trance-like state of euphoria.

Oliver, a gorgeous specimen of a child, hypnotic and handsome had come to mind, was followed by his grandparents, Mr and Mrs Turner. Ronny sighed with relief; her life hadn't just turned upside down. They all sat down around the table, joining her for a few hours of reminiscing and yet more coffee. She'd almost walked away and lost everything. Now, who was the fool?

Sarah could see the love in both their eyes and congratulated them. Oliver had wanted to go on the machine replicating a sports car, so he could drive it. Mrs Turner obliged, getting up to take him. She'd touched Ronny's hand as she'd passed her, indicating her approval with a huge smile. The embarrassment was written all over Ronny's face, but Martin had caught hold of her hand and kissed her on the cheek. She coloured even more after that.

Chapter Eighteen

Sunday morning hadn't got off to a good start. Ronny couldn't function at all. Everything she'd tried to do had ended up a disaster. The hoover had decided to blow out smoke rather than suck up the dust; she'd emptied the bag, it had been full. Plugging it in again, no sound at all. It had given up the ghost. Ronny had to resort to a dustpan and brush on her hands and knees.

Her mind was frazzled. A cup of hot tea had somehow ended up all over the coffee table, her clumsy actions causing the accident that could have caused more severe consequences; she could have spilt it all over herself. Removing the washed clothes from the dryer, the turquoise top she'd worn for the date at the Ness had shrunk, it was only fit for a midget now; she shouldn't have put it in the machine in hindsight. Reading the washing instructions had clearly clarified that, after the event. Annoyed, the top ended up in the bin.

A walk, she'd decided and a meal in the local public house, a roast beef dinner. Putting on her flat dolly shoes, a hole had appeared in the sole of the left shoe. The pair had added itself to the ruined top as she put on her comfy trainers instead. Her thin jacket, on close scrutiny, had required a much-needed wash. What the heck, Ronny, put it on anyway. She'd had enough.

As she walked out of the door, closing it behind her, the phone had rung. Ronny's tone of voice was out of character, a little hostile to be frank.

'Ouch, did you get out on the wrong side of the bed?' Martin asked. 'You sound slightly disgruntled.'

'Martin, I'm so pleased to hear your voice. Have I had a morning of it? Everything is going wrong, absolutely everything.' She'd meant it. The frustration was obvious.

'I'm almost finished taking Rufus for a walk. Where are you? I can meet you if you want.'

'How does Sunday lunch in the pub sound? That's where I'm heading for,' Ronny had replied.

'I'm on my way back from Teignmouth now. Give me half an hour and I will meet you there, okay. You can tell me all about your morning.' Martin hung up, blowing a kiss down the line.

Ronny smiled for the first time since waking up.

Noticing Jane and her husband, a colleague from the nursery, sat at one of the tables near the window, Ronny acknowledged her with a wave and headed for the bar. A large latte was ordered as she walked over to a vacant table, her usual one being occupied, typical, her luck was definitely non-existent today. The public house wasn't full, but people were scattered about the area, eating and conversing happily amongst themselves. Enjoying their Sunday, a day of rest, supposedly.

Martin walked in, looking around for her, eventually noticing her at the far end of the building.

He kissed her on the cheek before heading for the bar to order a drink. 'Shall I order the beef dinners while I'm up there?'

'Yes, please. I'm paying though, it's my turn.' Martin hadn't argued.

As he returned with a pint of lager, a smile erupted from her face. Martin had asked what had tickled her. She'd glanced over to where Jane and her husband were seated, ogling them both with curiosity. Ronny turned her back, avoiding the interested glares.

'We've been rumbled. The staff at work were wondering about us anyway, Martin. Jack guessed and I swore him to secrecy on Tuesday. Peter, my stepfather, had an inclination that something was going on between us and Mark was fishing for details yesterday. With Jane and her husband here, all of Shaldon will be talking about us.' Ronny smiled at the audience.

'Let them. You're not ashamed of me, are you?'

'Of course not. I wasn't sure whether you'd wanted us being the talk of the town this soon. I've tried to be discreet, honestly.' Ronny had offered. 'Talk of the devil, look who's just walked in.'

Martin turned around as Jack and Charlie had entered the premises, their eyes on Ronny and Martin straight away. She'd had no choice but to acknowledge them both. Sunday was usually a quiet affair, not seeing a soul. A ghost town out of season. What had happened today? The hysterics had started, Ronny couldn't stop herself.

She spoke about her catastrophes in the morning, now seeing the funny side of it all. A ruined top, worn-out shoes, an old hoover needing replacement. It wasn't that big an ordeal, not in the context of things: all material things that could be easily replaced. A wash cycle would put right her soiled coat; it hadn't been that dramatic at all. It had just felt like it at that precise moment in time.

The food arrived and was eaten quickly. The public house was renowned for its Sunday roasts, always of a high standard. As the customers left for their homes, Martin glanced at his watch.

Ronny wondered what time the boys would be returning from Bristol. Had they still had time to talk? She'd wanted to fill him in on Mark and his daughter, Abbie. It had been time he'd known about the new member of the family.

'It's okay; they're not due back yet. Are you okay now, Ronny?' He held her hand lovingly, a smile adorning his face.

'Yes, thanks to you. What would I do without you? Are we up for a shopping trip next week, for my wedding outfit? The choice of the shopping area is up to you, Martin. Your choice this time.'

'I will hold you to that. I love you, Ronny. I can't help it. Don't leave me, will you!' he said to her, concerned and so serious.

'Are you ready for the questions from the village residents? Tongues will be wagging, big time now. I don't care though. I love you, too.' She'd meant it. A round of applause had been heard from the adjacent table. One occupied by Jack and Charlie, Jack never missed a thing. Ronny coloured bright red and Martin kissed her in full view of the visitors still there. Whatever had happened to the wallflower of the village, she'd long gone now, and not by personal choice initially.

Heading towards the bakery shop, as Martin headed home to greet his twin boys, Ronny's mood had changed completely. Things to do had entered her brain, in an orderly fashion. Ensuring that Peter had condensed fully the information given to him the other day, of Abbie's existence basically, she climbed the stairs to the flat. They could be on another walk, but she'd wanted to check that he was okay, if he'd been there.

The "oldies" hadn't ventured out. Voices were heard from the living room, over and above Margaret and Peter's. As she walked into the room, Mark was sat on the sofa, talking business with his father, Peter. Margaret was talking to Lillian, planning the culinary delights for the bakery shop for the oncoming week.

'Hi, all. I'm putting the kettle on. Who's up for a cuppa?' Ronny shouted for all to hear. Four hands were raised, the children at the nursery had sprung to mind, and she inwardly sniggered. *We are all children at heart*, she'd thought to herself. Her mood had changed from glum to excitement. Martin always brought the best out in her.

With their individual discussions out of the way, a combined conversation began, about anything and everything. Margaret had asked whether she had eaten.

'Yes, thanks. I had a Sunday roast in the public house with Martin.' It had come out, not intentional. Oops!

Lillian looked at her, studying her expression. 'What, my Martin?'

It was out of the bag now, better to come from her than the local gossipers. 'Yes, Lillian. Your Martin.' Lillian had frozen; words had her dumbfounded.

202

'I knew it,' Peter piped up. 'Didn't I tell you, Margaret?' He had, after her last visit. Certain that there was chemistry between them at the last taster session.

'Well done, Sis. You could have told me yesterday, you know. I wouldn't have said a word.' His expressions had told a different story, though. She couldn't have trusted him any further than she could throw him.

'Well, Jack and Jane from work know now, so expect a lot of gossipers in your shop tomorrow, Mum.' Ronny was elated. 'Better you all hear it from the horse's mouth first.'

Margaret walked into the kitchen, returning with a large bottle of white wine and five glasses.

Handing a full glass to everyone there, she raised her glass for all to follow. 'Here's to finding Abbie, and Ronny and Martin's relationship.' It was getting to be a bit of a habit. Smiles adorned the faces of all there, including Lillian.

It had been time for Margaret and Lillian to return to their individual kitchens, cooking for the community, the popular bakery shop. Peter had wanted to sort out the paperwork for the business and put an order in for food for the shop, so Ronny put on her coat, heading for the front door.

'There's a state that coat is in, Veronica. Is your washing machine working?' Typical for Margaret to notice. Ronny smirked, not letting her mother see it.

'Yes, it is, Mum. I will see you all soon. Have a good journey back to Exeter tomorrow, if I don't see you before you go, Mark.' Ronny walked out of the door, beaming with happiness.

Walking back to the apartment, she spoke to Martin, informing him of her blunder, letting his mother know of their relationship. He'd sounded relieved, at least he'd not needed to tell her himself now. With the wedding date very close, she'd asked if he would be able to escort her if Matt and Rose could add another place to the reception at short notice.

'I'm sure I could sort something out with the boys. Susan could drop them off at The Devon Arms on Sunday, and we could all head back here together. You need to square things up with your stepbrother first.' Martin had replied.

'I'm onto it soon. I'm just walking through my front door. Speak to you later, say hello to Ben and Aaron for me.' Ronny put the phone down and was onto her usual routine. Putting the kettle on for a cuppa!

Matt answered the phone in such a relaxed fashion; nothing ever seemed to faze him.

Probably the clown of the two of them, Mark and Matt were very similar, personality-wise. He congratulated her on her detective work, in finding Pollianna's daughter and indeed Mark's, as well. His brother had updated him on it all, and he appeared as excited as Mark was.

'So, what do I owe the pleasure, Sis? How can I assist you this fine evening?'

'How did you know I wanted something? I could have just been phoning you for an update on life in London in general.' She wasn't though. 'Am I that transparent? Obviously so.'

'Out with it, girl.' Matt said, laughing.

'Is it too late for you to add a person to the reception? He can share my room at the venue.' There, she sighed a deep breath.

'I don't see an issue. What's his name, Ronny?'

Ronny told him and added the fact that they were in a relationship. Informing Matt that he was a native to Shaldon, Matt suddenly went quiet.

204

'Hold on, Martin Davies, quite a common name I know. I had someone working in my office of that name. He left a while ago, to pursue a new challenge in his birth town and to look after his children. Apparently, his partner had shacked up with another man.' Say it as it is, why don't you. That was Matt in a nutshell.

Ronny was intrigued and wanted to know more. She'd not known the nature of Matt's career in London, or Martin's whilst there, come to that. There hadn't been a need to know, not in all honesty. Highways and maintenance was an important business, apparently. The upkeep of busy motorways, urgent repairs and the innovative resurrection of new roads to allow people to travel anywhere and everywhere their lives had taken them. With new lives being born every minute, keeping up with living requirements was paramount and crucial in today's hectic world.

Ronny couldn't drive and had no aspiration to do so. Life on the road was chaotic, too much for her, in her own little bubble. Nevertheless, their jobs were important in these times, she'd not doubted. Had Martin worked with Matt in London? It had sounded plausible, they would soon find out, wouldn't they? With the formalities pencilled in, Matt hadn't envisaged any problems adding Martin to the guest list. Niceties were spoken about, Rose's bump and ensuring that Matt was taking good care of her. Ronny hung up. Another brew was required, she was parched. Music, Elvis particularly, was put on and she sat on the sofa with her tea and biscuits, almost falling asleep. The day had been a long, complicated one, but one she wouldn't have missed for the world.

Waking up with a jolt, Ronny searched in her dresser for a writing pad and a pen. The list in her head had included writing to her father, Vernon. A visit to the bathroom to freshen up, change into her pyjamas, and she was on the case. The dressing gown, her favourite, fluffy teddy bear material, was put on and she headed for the balcony to concentrate.

The wording had to be right, nothing detrimental to put him off. Margaret's take on what had happened, in all probability wasn't identical to his. Perceptions weren't always as clear cut as they'd looked. Ronny knew that from experience, she'd completely misread Martin and Sarah's closeness in Teignmouth. She could easily have lost him forever.

Pages were written and discarded, knowing that the words hadn't sounded how she'd wanted to portray things. Eventually, after juggling sentences, altering words and phrases, Ronny signed it by her true name, Veronica, and sealed it in an envelope, writing the address on the front of it. That was the best she could do. Hopefully, her dad would want to see her again and respond with some sort of communication. Her fingers were crossed behind her back as she'd uttered the words loudly. Would all her prayers come at once, she'd so hoped so. In bed, that night, her thoughts were muddled. Attention wasn't something Ronny was used to in her short life. Hiding behind a book in school, not a prominent partygoer and happy to accept her own company, her life was changing completely, way out of proportion.

Veronica Johnson had one breed to thank for it, men! Matt, Mark, Martin and Jack: all instrumental in the changes recently, not forgetting two scrumptious twin boys, Ben and Aaron. She'd never despised the male sex at all; the few dates over the years had been okayish. Nothing outstanding or enlightening and she had continued with her life devoid of the species, as a close contact in any case. She'd not had a father figure to look up to, either, more is the pity.

The thunderbolt of the past few weeks, and that's what the weeks were, a mixture of thunder and lightning, creating havoc around her safe little existence. A bolt out of the blue on meeting up with Matt, only to discover he was, in fact, Peter's son. She'd been impressed with his personification that was all masculine, his handsome face, his laughable character, and the almost immediate rapport they'd had, as complete strangers; all after her making a complete fool of herself in the public house. He would have become a good friend if they'd not been related. She'd no doubt about that.

Mark, on the other hand, hadn't appeared quite so forthcoming, at first. An identical twin, though Ronny could differentiate between them almost immediately, even stood up against one another. Mark, still a jovial human being in character, had required time to analyse the people he'd met, before bearing his soul, unlike his brother. Once certain of Ronny's character, asking her to find Abbie, his daughter, had realised his complete and utter confidence in her as a person. He'd trusted her implicitly.

Jack, the male equivalent of an adorable female human being, was as close to an old school friend that she could ever hope to meet. His worrying over her in the nursery, the obvious nerves, apparent to him, that no one there would have ever even noticed. He mollycoddled her as if she was his little sister, wanting only the best for her in life. His excitement at realising hers and Martin's relationship was actually flourishing, had held no bounds. She wanted him there, as a permanent part of her life, though on a completely different level altogether.

Martin was her soul mate, a new relationship, admittedly. He was the glue that was holding her together, the shoulder to cry on and the father of her favourite little beings at the nursery. She had not wanted to admit to having favourites, all children were infectious little beings in reality. Little Abbie was an angel that she'd wanted to get to know a lot more, and nothing was going to stop her on that score.

Martin had brought out senses that she'd not known existed in her body, she'd dreamt of being with him forever and ever. Life wasn't like that though, but Ronny was going to do her damnedest to ensure that that had become a realisation for the future and beyond, if at all possible. Fires did burn out, nothing is guaranteed. It was indeed a scary thought, but one well worth pursuing.

Her father, Vernon, was the unknown entity, as yet to rediscover. Her memories as a child, it was all good, but now she wanted to get to know the person that had brought her into this world and had loved her mother throughout the time they'd spent together. Things hadn't turned out as planned, life had taken a U-turn, but that wasn't to say the future couldn't include the man in her life she had needed to pursue, her dad, had it?

Ronny had slept well that night, really well. Elvis Presley was her idol, the most handsome man that had ever walked this earth, with a voice no one could ever better. His poster was displayed secretly inside her bathroom cabinet, her guilty obsession (Don't tell anyone). But he was dead, leaving this earth far too soon. His memory will live on forever, in his music, to that there's no illusion, none whatsoever.

The men in her life were here now, causing untold chaos to her usually hermit-style existence. Ronny wouldn't have had it any other way. She was in heaven, euphorically. Life couldn't be so good, and it was getting even better, something or someone from up above was telling her. Elvis had whispered it in her ear, just then, before she'd nodded off completely.

Chapter Nineteen

Ronny posted the letter to Vernon, her dad, on the way to work on Monday morning. She'd so hoped her words had made the impact on her father that had been intended. It was out of her hands now, the next move was up to him, and him alone. No one could blame him for turning away from his past completely.

As she walked into the nursery, all eyes were upon her. Where was Jack when she wanted him for support? Jack walked in a few minutes afterwards. 'Help me,' she said to him. 'I feel like I'm in a goldfish bowl.'

'Leave this to me, Ronny,' Jack had replied, before heading towards the other staff members and speaking to them privately. What he had said to them, she'd not known, but it had worked. All workstations returned to normal as the children entered the nursery.

Martin walked in with the boys and they jabbered on about their weekend with their mum and Craig, full of excitement. 'We went to the zoo, Miss. The big monkey was playing with a football, just like Ben and I do,' Aaron had said to her.

'That was good. I'm glad you had a nice time.' They both headed towards the painting table, already set up with everything required. There would be a lovely mess to clear up at lunchtime, but children and paint went together perfectly. The budding artists loved experimenting.

Martin had sensed that the atmosphere was different, asking if all was okay with her. Ronny nodded negatively. Eyes were on Martin, all so apparent. 'Leave this to me.' He walked over to the staff manager, requesting a word in private. On leaving to go to work, he winked to Ronny as he walked out of the door.

Lunchtime had Jack escorting her to the public house for a coffee. Martin had told it as it was to the most senior person of the nursery. Susan had walked out on him, after conducting an affair whilst he was working away during the week. She was now living in Bristol with him and he was there for the boys on a permanent basis. Ronny's friendship had become personal only after Susan had left. She hadn't broken them up. Ronny was not to be gossiped about in any context, him either.

Jane, the female worker had a lot to answer for. No wonder Ronny had preferred the companionship of men. The male sex was far less prone to gossip, all good. They'd not had a lot of time to enjoy the coffee, but she was more than grateful to Jack for taking her away from the morning's trivialities. Tuesday's now regular tête-à-tête was more than looked forward to tomorrow. Would Ronny be attending the Wednesday curry house evening meal in Teignmouth? Yes, she'd told Jack, absolutely. He would be there to take care of her, and she'd done nothing wrong, except fall in love. Back to work she went and things were more or less back to normal. When Martin had called to collect the boys, Ronny had given him the thumbs up, indicating that his word with the head had worked.

What a day! Ronny engaged in checking online for a new hoover. She could have browsed the shops on the weekend for one, but a wedding outfit was to be purchased then, and she hadn't wanted to wait a further week. Brushing up had been okay temporarily, but not all the time. She'd had savings put by to afford one, in any case.

Martin had phoned her each evening; the gossipmongers had stopped spreading untruths and had gotten fed up of finding out that the people they'd spoken to had already been informed of Martin and Ronny's intimate friendship. They'd all wanted to be first in spreading the news. Martin had spoken to the boys, telling them that their daddy was seeing Miss on weekends when they were with Mummy and Craig. They'd taken it well, with a "We like Miss, Daddy". Enough said.

Wednesday's curry night had Jane apologising to Ronny profusely. With the words obviously coming directly from her, she'd been reprimanded by the staff manager and ordered to put things right between all the staff members. Spreading gossip wasn't something the nursery was there for, looking after the children being the priority. The evening had been enjoyed by all, afterwards.

Margaret had called, checking on her. Customers to her shop had almost doubled over the week, all wanting to know if the romantic liaison was true. Her mother's answer had a simple reply. She wasn't her daughter's keeper and at 30 years of age hadn't followed her around. If they'd wanted to know anything, better ask Veronica herself. The customers had walked out of the shop with a flea in their ear, discovering absolutely nothing. Well done, Mother.

It was Saturday, and Ronny was meeting Martin at the café as usual. Where he was taking her, she'd no idea. The wedding invitation had now included Martin, whether he had needed new clobber, he'd not said. The compulsory beverage in the café had started their day, how it was going to end, could be anybody's guess. Shopping, in general, was never something Ronny had made a habit of.

Getting in the car, Martin headed for the motorway, driving until signs for Exeter were seen clearly in view. He'd pulled off the motorway, driving to Exeter's town centre. Asking whether Martin had shopped there on a regular basis, the answer had been a negative one. The shops were plentiful, he'd responded. An outfit would be found in such a large vicinity of shopping facilities. He'd presumed correctly if Ronny couldn't find anything in the numerous clothes shops there, she'd no hope.

Debenhams had started her search, but all outfits had felt a bit too frumpy on her, adding years to her age. Martin had turned his nose up at all she'd tried on. Miss Selfridge and Wallis had received similar vibes. An outfit in Peacocks, a mediocre chain of shops, had shown an outfit on a mannequin in the window. Ronny's eyes were immediately drawn to it. 'That's what I want, Martin,' she said.

They'd walked into the shop, found her size, Ronny heading for the fitting room. Her reflection in the mirror had received a resounding yes. Showing Martin before removing the shift dress and short-sleeved bolero, his thumbs up had agreed with her decision. Now for a handbag and shoes. The handbag had just appeared there, in front of her, as she'd stood in the queue to pay for the outfit. Two out of three, one more purchase to make.

Food and a cup of tea urgently needed. A Wetherspoons establishment had been espied, that would do perfectly. Ronny so wanted a sit-down and sighed as she'd found a suitable seat. The lunchtime menu was admirable, inexpensive and tasty. Neither of them had any complaints. Two cups of tea followed.

'Do you need to buy anything for the wedding, Martin? I just want shoes now, but I can always get those in Teignmouth if nothing is found here. I've got the important piece of clothing.' Ronny was getting excited about the event now.

'My work suit, white shirt and good tie will suffice. None of it is that old. I worked in an office in London, remember,' he'd answered.

'So you did. Is there anything else you need to purchase here in Exeter?' Ronny asked.

'Yes, there is actually. Come on, I know the shop exactly.' He waited for her to get up and pulled her to a shop opposite the Wetherspoons establishment: a jewellery shop. Glancing in the window, Ronny looked but hadn't registered why they were there.

'I want you to pick a ring, Ronny,' he said to her.

'I don't need a ring, Martin.' She'd not understood.

Martin caught hold of her left hand, pressing firmly on her wedding finger. He then looked directly at her. The penny had dropped.

'A ring on this finger will represent how I feel about you. It's not been long, I know, but my feelings aren't going to change in the future. Can I buy a ring for this finger, Ronny?' He'd not asked her to marry him outright, but she'd known exactly what he was saying.

Elvis had whispered in her ear, *It's Now or Never.* 'Yes,' she replied. 'Yes, I will marry you.' A kiss had followed before entering the jewellery shop, emerging from there with a sparkling piece on her wedding finger, and huge grins adorning both their faces. The elation was twofold.

She'd still not bought shoes, but they could wait, Ronny hadn't wanted to shop anymore. 'Can I ask a huge, ginormous favour, please?' she'd said, looking at him dolefully with huge puppy eyes. 'We're in Exeter and I have Dad's address here. Can you drive there; I would like to pay him a visit if only to see where he lives.'

Taking the piece of paper with an address on it, she handed it to him. He typed the postcode into the sat-nav and drove off. Although Exeter is a fairly large city, the journey hadn't taken that long. Ronny's memories of living there were more or less non-existent, having left there at the tender age of five. However, landmarks passed seemed familiar; remarking on them to Martin as he drove by 'It's just around the corner, my grandparents' house, I'm sure of it,' her head was telling her. 'On the left, just there, Martin.' Ronny was behaving like an over-excited child. Her arms and legs were going ten to the dozen.

Martin stopped, virtually opposite the house she'd mentioned. Ronny was right. Looking at him with joy at first, then nervous uncertainty, she asked him whether she should knock on the door.

'We're here now. A pity to waste the journey. I will stay here in the car. Holler if you need any help.' He kissed her on the cheek, pushing her out of the passenger door before she'd opted out.

Very steadily, Ronny walked down the short driveway. A council house it was, rented by her grandparents in the year dot, so long ago she couldn't remember precisely: a three-bedroomed, reasonably spacious property with a good-sized lounge and larger than average kitchen, as she'd remembered. The back garden was laid mainly to lawn with a concrete built shed at the bottom.

Her grandmother had loved her garden, and beds of various coloured bushes and arranged flowers were always being lovingly cared for. The lavender bush, its gorgeous smell and colour, had been her pride and joy. The dining table always included a vase of the purple flowers in the centre of it. The lounge had always smelled crisp and fresh because of them. No stuffiness, ever.

There had been a gooseberry bush at the bottom of the back garden. She'd recalled helping to pick them with her grandparents. Popping one into her mouth, the acidic taste had caused a face of utter dislike. She'd never eaten one again, one that hadn't been cooked, that was. The pies made from them were to die for, covered in bird's custard, thick and delicious. Visiting Grandma was always looked forward to, as children, as it should have been.

Ronny's grandmother was a good cook, always something in the oven or boiling in a pot on the gas hob. The pig's head one day when there, had boiled away for hours. She'd made her own brawn; Ronny hadn't liked the taste but hadn't known until after her parents had arrived home that that was what it was. 'Disgusting,' she had said to them when they'd informed her. They'd both laughed at her: children at their best.

Silly things had stuck in Ronny's head, buried for years. Now they were returning as she'd knocked on the front door. Apprehensively, she jumped when the door opened, standing there staring at the man in front of her. He hadn't changed, the added wrinkles, hair now grey and balding in places, but she would have recognised him anywhere.

'Dad,' she said nervously. 'It's Veronica.'

He was dumbfounded, stuck to the spot unable to move. His face was a picture of disbelief. 'Veronica, my little girl.'

'Not so little anymore, Dad. I'm 30 years old now, all grown up.' She caught his hand, steadying him: he'd looked as if he was going to fall. 'Can I come in?'

'Of course. Bring your friend, too.' He'd seen someone in the car opposite, staring over. Ronny signalled to Martin to join her. He turned the engine off and walked down the driveway. 'Come on in, both of you, please.' They both followed Vernon into the lounge. An elderly lady was sat in the chair nearest the electric fire, sleeping, Ronny had thought at first. She opened her eyes, looking towards them nervously.

'Who are you?' she asked. 'Vernon, who are these people?' She was becoming agitated.

'It's me, Grandma, Veronica. Your granddaughter,' she said softly, heading towards her.

'Veronica, my Veronica! Vernon, Veronica is here.'

'I know, Mother. I'm making tea for them now. Sit down, please,' he said to them both promptly.

They both sat on the sofa, Ronny glancing around the room. The photographs displayed reignited long-gone memories. Picking one up in particular, she passed it to Martin. 'There, that's my granddad. His name was Vernon

Victor senior. All our Christian names begin with a V. It's the law!' She was laughing as Vernon brought in the tea.

'Oh, I'd better remember that, hadn't I?' Martin was laughing, too.

'Here you are, Mother. A nice cup of tea for you.'

As if by premonition, Ronny hadn't known why she shouted out at exactly the same time as her grandmother had. 'Don't forget the biscuits, Vernon.' A huge grin crossed their faces.

She spoke for a long while with her dad, before introducing Martin to him. 'This is Martin, we've just got engaged, Dad.' Showing him her ring, he congratulated them both. 'Martin likes surprising me; I'd no clue today was going to happen.' She touched his hand affectionately and he smiled.

'Hello, Mr Johnson. Martin Davies, you don't remember me, do you?' He'd given Vernon something to think about, and he had for a good while, before replying.

'Your parents, Lillian and David, if I'm right. You've got a brother, Mark is it?' He was getting there.

'Michael, my brother is. You probably recall Sarah Turner and me skipping to school every morning holding hands. You used to be behind us, with Veronica and Virginia.' Martin had waited, for anything really.

'You were the naughty one, weren't you? Lillian was forever running after you, for something or other. I remember telling your mother that she'd have her hands full with you as you got to your teens.' His cogs were going, all recollections completely correct.

Ronny had gone into one of her fits of laughter; her sides were hurting, tears in her eyes. 'Trust me to pick the rebellious one, Dad.' Her hand was still holding her fiancé's, all joking aside.

They'd stayed there for over two hours until Martin had indicated that it was time to head back to Shaldon. It would be dark before they'd returned home, otherwise. Vernon hadn't wanted them to go, and her grandmother's odd small talk had implied a slight recollection of some events of the past.

The dementia was obvious, her grandmother was still there, though; the one Ronny had vivid memories of. The sweet little lady with a sometimes vicious tongue, not always meant the way it had been spoken. The love for all her family was indeed unconditional. Virginia, or Gina, would have many more incidents to recall, and Ronny had so wanted them both there now, reliving them together. Embracing both her grandmother and her father, she'd promised to visit again soon. She looked at Martin for confirmation, who had nodded positively.

'We will definitely return the visit. Your daughter doesn't drive, so it's up to me. She will have to learn, I'm thinking.' He hadn't appeared serious, thankfully. Ronny had screwed her nose up, the confidence or the yearning wasn't there, for her being behind a wheel. That was Gina's calling.

The waves, driving away, had caused Ronny to cry, happy tears. She became emotional all the way back home, tears streaming down her face. He'd stopped at the café, but she'd remained in the car, signalling him to park outside her apartment instead. He'd not argued with her.

'I need you with me, tonight,' she'd said. 'No more surprises though. I've no tears left to shed.' She hadn't.

Chapter Twenty

It was the night before Matt and Rose's wedding. Martin and Ronny had arrived at The Devon Arms safely and checked into their room. Nothing spectacular: a standard room with an en suite bathroom. The elation of having a bath and a shower had caused her to smile. Not all hotel rooms enjoyed both amenities; it was sometimes one or the other, but not always both of them.

There was a menu sat on the desk, with meals to eat in the room as well as in the dining room downstairs. Talking amongst themselves, they had decided on a meal in the room, a slushy film on the television and an early night. Martin had wholeheartedly agreed with her spoken choice for the evening, it had sounded heavenly. Time to themselves before meeting the whole family and the invited guests unknown to them.

Had Ronny had time for a bath? Yes, she'd decided, taking her pyjamas into the bathroom with her. She was going nowhere. Martin had settled himself comfortably on the bed, pillows plumped up enough to see the television clearly, playing about with the remote until a programme had taken his fancy. He'd ordered their meal. Beverages were there on the desk for them to prepare as and when they'd pleased.

A knock on their door, Martin had answered it, expecting their ordered meal. The face at the other side of the door had belonged to Matt, though. Ronny had just got out of the bath, having put her nightwear on. She walked out of the bathroom as the door had been opened.

'Hi, Matt. Come on in. We've ordered a take-in for tonight. How are you feeling?'

Matt hadn't answered her, staring at Martin. 'Hello, Martin. I had wondered whether the person Ronny spoke about was you. How are things going in the work area?'

'Mr Sutherland. You're Ronny's stepbrother?' He was lost for words. 'I'm loving the job, thanks, and being back in my comfort zone, my birth town.'

'You've picked a good one here, Sis. Martin excelled at his job with me. He is sorely missed. I don't suppose you'd like your old job back?' He was playing, Ronny knew him too well.

'Not a chance. I've got everything I want now: my twin boys, Ronny and home.' He'd spoken with complete honesty in his voice. 'I'm happy with my lot, sometimes too much responsibility and high salaries can cloud one's mind for a while.'

'Well said.' Matt suddenly noticed the diamond ring on Ronny's finger. 'Have you forgotten to mention something, Sis?' He waited patiently for a reply.

'Martin surprised me. There will be another wedding in the family, Matt. Mum is over the moon.' She glanced over at her fiancé and smiled at him, so happy.

Another knock at the door, this time it was their food. Matt said his goodbyes, leaving them to it. Were there to be any more surprises, he'd wondered.

An early morning start, the wedding was at eleven o'clock, followed by the reception and then the evening entertainment. Ronny had huffed and puffed, putting on her make-up and trying to do something different to her hair. The volume and thickness just caused any change in hairstyle to flop. Ronny's patience was at its lowest ebb, and the frustration had well gotten to her.

Ponytails wouldn't stay in that long, so a bun of sorts was out of the question. She'd eventually given up with an exasperated sigh, brushing it to its normal and boring, straight bob type style.

Martin's grin and her obvious efforts resulted in Ronny getting cross with him. A cushion was hurled through the air, aimed directly at him. It had missed abominably. The laughter had returned as Martin hugged her affectionately.

'Breath,' he'd instructed her. 'We've plenty of time. You look gorgeous in any case.'

'You're biased, your comments don't count. You would love me if I was dressed in a black bag, with long matted greasy hair.' The thought of it had made her squirm. Ronny's description had caused another roar from Martin. 'Stop, you'll ruin my make-up.'

Jewellery had been next on the list in her head. Having to shop for shoes in Teignmouth, Ronny had purchased a necklace and matching earrings, delicate and pretty, not expensive at all. It had looked impressive with her outfit, even if she'd said so herself. Turning to Martin she'd uttered, 'Well, do I scrub up okay?'

There were no words required. His expression had said it all. As they headed for the hotel lift to take them down to the ceremonial room, Ronny had felt so proud to be with Martin, linking arms as they seated themselves where the usher had sent them. Looking around, she could see familiar faces. Gina, Alastair and the twins were sat in the row behind her, and Mark and little Abbie were nearby. She'd waved at her, Abbie waving back excitedly. Peter and Margaret were at the front, Ronny's mother had looked lovely.

Behind her, a family were seated. There had been no doubt in her mind. It was Luke, Miriam and Simon. Matt and Mark's brother was unmistakable, the likeness uncanny. She would speak to them at the reception, a requirement to suss out the other brother and his personality traits. Another addition to her now extended family.

At the other side of the room were people she'd not known, obviously Rose's family and friends of them both. Glancing around twice, astounded at first, she'd got up running across the aisle. 'Dad, what are you doing here?'

'Your mother and Peter invited me. It was supposed to be a surprise for you and Virginia, but that didn't go accordingly, did it?' Vernon had dressed up well, looking smart and pristine.

'Well, I wouldn't have seen Grandma then, would I?' Ronny's answer had been completely true. She'd given him a huge hug.

The music had started, so Ronny returned to her designated seat quickly. Rose had dressed appropriately, the bump unavoidable but graciously covered in cream silk and delicate lace. On her head a simple veil beginning at the back of her ponytailed hair, reaching the floor far behind her. Ronny could have cried happy tears but remembered her make-up and somehow managed to control herself. Martin had sensed her emotions, holding her hand throughout the short ceremony. Wow, the sentimental words the couple had spoken to one another, before the wedding rings were exchanged, had Ronny reaching for her handkerchief. It had been too late, the mascara evident on the cottoned fabric. Martin sorted it out before any of the guests had noticed. He couldn't help but kiss her on the cheek afterwards.

Matt's grin whilst walking past everyone, with Rose by his side, was euphoric, he'd beamed with delight. He'd met his soulmate and now they were joined in matrimony, with a lovely little bundle on the way soon. The cheers from the guests had sealed their love, hopefully forever. 'We're next,' Martin had whispered in her ear.

At the reception, at the head table, all the "oldies" were there proud as ever. Peter and Vernon spoke openly to one another, with no hostility whatsoever. Vernon hadn't found another lady to take Margaret's place, but he'd been perfectly content with his life. His daytime job and his mother had kept him busy, for sure. He'd no interest in looking for a partner unless fate had chosen something in the future. Who knew, his lady friend could still be out there, waiting.

Margaret had equally engaged in small talk with her ex-husband. No arguments, just pure elation and joy at the happy occasion. The day was everything it should be and more. Virginia had spent hours with Vernon after the reception, introducing Jenny and Jonathan as his grandchildren, and her husband, Alastair. He'd been absolutely overwhelmed. An initial reference to their Christian names though had caused concern, at first.

'Their full names are Victor Jonathan and Violet Jennifer, Dad. I hadn't forgotten.' Her dad's face had brightened, adding a sincere thank you from him.

Rose had introduced Ronny to her brother, John. A smirk had erupted, thinking about Matt's hope in linking them together, before Martin had come into the equation and onto the scene. He wasn't her type at all. Handsome, yes, no question on that score. But his personality had hinted at snobbery, nothing wrong with that in itself if the boot had fitted. Ronny's match though, absolutely not! She'd found her perfect partner, at long last. He'd been there all along, at Teignmouth high school. The Casanova of the classroom, now content with the wallflower of Shaldon, Veronica Johnson. How people changed over the years.

Little Abbie had looked like a princess. Her long floaty dress, bought by her grandparents, Mr and Mrs Burns. Her hair had cute curls falling from her blond hair, a hairband complimenting the dress, completing the outfit. She'd held onto her dad's hand throughout the ceremony but was now sat on a chair talking to Peter and Margaret, completely at home with them.

Rose's parents had spoken to everyone there, as did Rose's friends and a few of Matt's work colleagues, who'd been invited, some familiar to Martin. He'd happily spent time filling them in on his new life back home. Patting him on the back, they'd commended him on pursuing his true vocation in life. Money had often stopped people from taking the course he had. Finances often wouldn't allow it. Martin had been lucky there.

'When is your wedding going to happen?' All were asking.

'Give us a chance,' Ronny had answered them all. 'We've only just got engaged.'

'Soon' had been the reply from Martin. Soon. Nothing concrete had had time to be discussed as yet, but soon had sounded good, in Ronny's eyes. They would be busy sorting things out after all had died down. Nothing too big, the occasion for Matt and Rose's day was perfection in itself.

Another night in the hotel had all meeting up that morning, saying their goodbyes. With Luke, Miriam and Simon remaining in the UK for another two weeks, a promise of meeting up at The Ness for a proper chat was on the cards very soon. Their little village of Shaldon had sounded idyllic. They wouldn't miss a few days vacating there between seeing family members, old and new.

Mark was now well established in Teignmouth. His restaurant was doing well, with Ronny's help. Everyone in her vicinity had received a flyer advertising his new restaurant near the ferry port. She couldn't sing his praises enough. Occasional nights working there was still being done by Ronny, but the staffing levels were almost where Mark had wanted them now. Margaret's dark orange chocolate cake was an astounding success and a permanent addition to the bakery shop and the dessert menu at Mark's restaurant. She'd loved helping out if she'd been truthful.

The little house at number 12 was prettied up by Ronny. The smaller bedroom now occupied unicorn memorabilia in bundles and a pretty unicorn duvet (Ronny was jealous). Abbie's bedroom when she stayed there, which had now become more frequent. Mr and Mrs Burns were able to engage in a night, without worrying about their granddaughter. Mark's establishment had often included them treating themselves to a meal on Mark's day off.

Peter and Margaret would often be seen escorting three lively children to the local park on a Sunday afternoon after Susan had brought them back from Bristol that was: Abbie, Ben and Aaron.

They all got along famously together, with the odd argument over children's toys and whose turn it was to push the roundabout. There were enough swings there to accommodate all three of them when the playground wasn't full of other children.

Matt and Rose had made a visit to Shaldon, staying with Mark, as opposed to The Ness. Abbie's bedroom had doubled up as a nursery when they were there. They'd brought the newly born baby to the nursery where Ronny had worked. Introducing the little bundle to her and everyone else there as Maggie, she was so scrumptious, Ronny was definitely broody now.

Magdalene Evelyn Mary was the baby's full name, all from the Bible. No one in the nursery had understood Ronny's expression when Matt had told her, but she'd loved her name, she really had.

The arrangements for the wedding were almost completed; The Ness being the obvious establishment for the occasion, Ronny's favourite. Not quite as many guests as Matt and Rose had had in Exeter, but enough to make the day special. The hotel, similar to The Devon Arms had conducted wedding ceremonies there, so all was done in one place, perfect.

Ronny hadn't wanted an ornate celebration, no balloons or streamers; the dining room in the hotel was to remain the same, nothing added. Simplicity in itself. Abbie, Ben and Aaron were to be bridesmaid and page boys. Jenny and

Jonathan were in charge of handing out the confetti after the ceremony was finished. Little Maggie was too small at the moment, and Simon had nodded in disagreement when asked if he'd wanted to be included.

Ronny's dress was simple but beautifully put together. Her hairstyle was not changed, a small tiara encrusted with sparkling stones adding that little bit of luxury to the boring hair she could do nothing with. Martin had surprised her with a white gold necklace and earrings for the day, small and unique, she had loved the jewellery.

She'd handed in her notice on her apartment, as she was moving into Martin's house after the wedding. She would miss it, she knew, but there had been no need for it afterwards. The family house was there waiting for her, Martin's childhood home. Everything had slowly moved from hers to his in a day, leaving the minimum effects remaining to take back after the wedding. She'd still had a few days left on the contract, so there had been no immediate urgency there. Her balcony had a last long session the night before, a glass of wine (not a bottle) accompanying her on the patio table.

Her apartment had recalled lots of good memories, but there were more memories in the pipeline, more responsibility too. The first port of call would be learning from her mother, Margaret. She'd had the urgency to be able to bake, her mother's art, and to appease three other appetites, Martin, Ben and Aaron's. It had suddenly become important to her, very important.

The nursery staff, from becoming a hive for gossip at the beginning, were now celebrating with them both, as excited as she was at the oncoming day of the wedding. Ronny had initially wanted to exclude them all, except Jack of course, who Martin had asked to be his best man, but couldn't.

She'd forgiven them for their indiscretions.

The children had busied themselves with painting pictures of a bride and groom, all put on the wall of the nursery for everyone to see. Their concentration at drawing Martin and Ronny was endearing, they'd all wanted to do a nice picture. Ronny could have cried every time she'd walked past them, admiring their attempts.

The wedding cake was made, by none other than her mother, but a "proper" cake as Martin had echoed. His dislike of having a ginormous dark orange chocolate cake adorning the wedding table had him having nightmares. Ronny had spared him that, laughing at him in the process. She had though, unbeknown to Martin, had her make a small one, for the evening entertainment afterwards.

Margaret was sworn to secrecy, it was a surprise, and her idea of a joke, a tasty addition to the buffet food later on in the day.

The executive suite had been booked, and paid for, by Matt. His treat, he'd said on telling them.

The best room in the hotel, especially for her. How she had loved her newfound family: Ronny couldn't believe it. The room at the back of the hotel, overlooking the fabulous views, would be hers and Martin's for the night. Mark was having the boys staying over with him.

'There is a surprise for you too, Sis,' Matt had said. 'You'll find out on the evening.'

'Thank you, you've got me wondering now.' A bottle of the best bubbly had come to mind, or something similar. Matt was an old romantic at heart.

Ronny's dad was to walk her down the aisle, giving her away. He couldn't have been happier, an honour for him. Her grandmother, due to her dementia, wasn't able to be there. Vernon had ensured there was a carer present, looking after her throughout the night and most of the next day. Everything was ready for their special day.

The day had gone perfectly, with no hiccups at all. A little nervous, Ronny was, but other than that, it was perfection in itself.

Martin had sent shivers down her spine as she'd entered the ceremonial room with her father. He was 100% her match and looked handsome in his dark suit and silk tie. As they walked back down the aisle together, now a couple legally, the confetti was thrown over them, it hadn't been a dream. This was real. Veronica Davies was a new person, nothing like her former self. She'd long gone.

The first dance had to be an Elvis number, no question there. But, as they stood in the centre of the dance floor, it wasn't *It's Now or Never* playing, but the song *Don't*. The words had fitted the occasion perfectly. The "oldies" were singing the song, over and above Elvis's voice. He would still be her heartthrob; nothing was ever going to change that.

As the night ended and the newly married couple retreated to the executive suite, the one her stepbrother had paid for, Ronny's eyes almost popped out of her head. The room was absolutely stunning, all she'd ever expected. There was no champagne or flowers, her surprise from Matt hadn't been that. So, what was it then?

As she walked onto the balcony, initially to admire the views over Shaldon, Teignmouth and beyond, there was something in the corner. Ronny walked over to it, removing the cloth covering it. There, in all its glory, was a large easel, complete with paint and paintbrushes. Matt's idea of a joke, but her obsession to paint the fabulous scenery, was still there in her mind. One day, she uttered to herself, one day!

Ronny had something to say to Martin that night, a secret she'd hidden from everyone for a few weeks. Her anxiousness had become apparent to him; she couldn't keep much from her husband.

'Spit it out, Veronica,' he'd said, copying her mother's stern voice of authority.

'I'm pregnant, Martin. You're going to be a daddy again.' Ronny waited for a response, good or bad.

He was so excited, hysterically so. 'We'd better start thinking about Christian names now; there are not that many beginning with a V.'